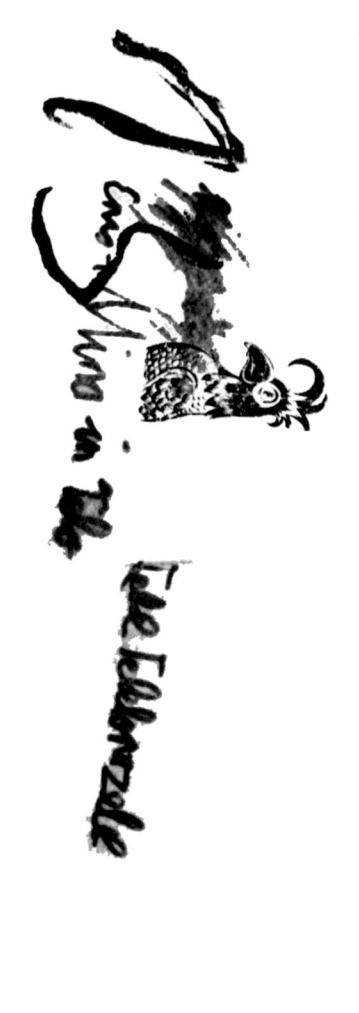

<u>Purchasing options</u>

Satellites Mistaken for Stars
I am talking about the interforms of communication /
the interstages of thought / I am talking about the
intercultures of emotion / why shouldn't that be the
only world. 68)

A book published in 2010 by *rupa publishing*.
ISBN 1-58423-225-0

Everybody get out of the pool
We didn't create an alternative culture. We were
mainstream parasites. 69)

A series of zines, in a limited edition of 100 each,
self-published, 2007—2009.

1+1=3
Insertions in Automated Visual Routines
Masking a basic reality in order to provoke a reflection
on the absence of a basic reality.

wear T-shirts that turn them into advertising bill-boards. He likes empty rooms that are white, because they allow space for things to happen. For that reason he has lived in the same featureless and nearly empty flat for years, because he finds it easier to get some rest without pictures on the wall. He listens to music preferably moving from room to room or with the windows open, in order to feel the differences when the sound mixes with the atmosphere of the room or the noise from outdoors. He likes playing the guitar on a 15V amplifier in his living room with the TV on but muted. If he can complain from time to time about the bad and wicked world in general, that puts him in a good mood. For years he has not slept a whole night through and has frequently been dreaming of plane crashes lately. He thinks he has a lot of useless knowledge about a lot of things nobody is interested in. He likes the summer, but dislikes swimming trunks and shorts – or maybe it is just his pale legs. He loves the stage between sleeping and being awake, when thoughts and images come to one's mind from nowhere in a half-aware, accidental order to create strange combinations. He is still nervous in front of a stage after having seen far more than a thousand bands play. He has been known to cry at the beauty of a song or a piece of art. He hates crowds of people, the mediocrity of format radio that only operates according to the principle of minimal unpopularity, re-lationships initiated over the internet, marketing and sales concepts, people talking on their mobiles in public, and a lot of other things too. He immediately falls asleep while watching any sort of sport on television. He usually reads four to five books at the same time and in quick rotation. He has always tried to maintain a degree of independence and therefore maintains a certain distance from associations or movements.

He sees the course of life as unstable, un-determined, and fraught with incalculable risks: at any moment a life can undergo a radical, uncontrollable change. How one's actions are valued is mainly beyond one's power and control. Hope and confidence are necessary to cope with the requirements of life.

Deutsche Bibliothek. Die Deutsche Bibliothek lists this publication in the Deutsche National-bibliografie; detailed bibliographic data is available in the Internet at http://dnb.ddb.de.

Design and concept
Alexander Egger

Text editor and translations as indicated
Edita Nosowa

www.satellitesmistakenforstars.com
www.rupapublishing.com

67)
Georgia O'Keeffe

<u>Where I was born and where and how I have lived is unimportant. It is what I have done with where I have been that should be of any interest.</u> 67)

When the viewer finds him or herself in a situation where he or she does not have to deal with an amount of obvious explanations and suggestions from the author to start with, he is challenged to estimate for him or herself to what extent he is attracted by something. The temptation to view this work as a consequence of certain aspects of the author's personality or biography is replaced by a mostly unencumbered view. The possibility given the recipient to match the images in the book with the images in his or her head extends the testimony and the meaning offered in the work. The concept of subjectivity is removed by a system of intersubjective relationships between single individuals. An intermediate layer, an associational interface that is both social and political, could ideally be established, allowing the personal psychological sensitivities of the creator to vanish.

65)
Jim Jarmusch

Whoever still feels the urge to learn some biographical details about Alexander Egger can find them in the following random outline, in the exact order they entered his mind on 1 November 2007.

Until the age of six he was left-handed. He is not easily impressionable, but can fall in love with the beauty of incidental movements certain people make which are not intended for anyone in particular. Discontentment with his own inadequacies is a strong motivation and driving force for him. His output is determined by shyness, probably because he originally comes from a very small place in the middle of the Alps. Since that time, however, he has learned to circulate in the anonymity of big cities with a certain implicitness.

66)
Rainald Goetz: *Abfall für alle*, 1989.
Material.

<u>Nothing is original. Steal from anywhere that resonates with inspiration or fuels your imagination. Devour old films, new films, music, books, paintings, photographs, poems, dreams, random conversations, architecture, bridges, street signs, trees, clouds, bodies of water, light and shadows. Select only things to steal that speak directly to your soul. If you do this, your work (and theft) will be authentic. Athenticity is invaluable; originality is non-existent.</u> 65)

Every reasonable attempt has been made to identify the owners of copyrights. All errors or omissions will be corrected in subsequent editions.

The title: *we have no scar to show for happiness* is a quotation from Chuck Pahlaniuk: *Diary*. The topic of the book is inspired by the early work of Rainald Goetz. 66)

First published in 2010. Printed in Europe.
ISBN: 978-3-940393-17-3

Single episodes become interwoven and associated with one another in terms of meaning in order to fabricate a continuity of life, which forms the basis for the development of identity. A consolidation of the memories is reached through frequently invoking these basic patterns, which continually undergo change. Internal breaks are filled up with adapted and appropriated external material, whose sources are often unclear or not remembered.

What in one's mind seems to be a genuine and original memory is often supplemented by vague and uncertain material, not even experienced by oneself but borrowed from unreliable sources. Memory is not an exact and precisely stable reservoir of experiences: it could be better described as a constructive framework that does not simply portray reality, but constantly filters and interprets the manifold and complex causalities of function. Evoking memories consists in activating associative and connotative patterns. Authentic reproduction of and fidelity to the original proves to be secondary when the activation of those single fragments of memory is in a constant state of mutation in order to maintain the continuity of one's life. The representation of experiences in one's mind is based on multimodal patterns of very different parts and combinations of single entities of experience.

Every activation of a memory vivifies and strengthens the brain's neuronal connections and saves the memory from fading or becoming lost; but at the same time it constructs, remodels, and reconnects these particles of memory. Social interaction, transmission of knowledge, and communication both cause and are subjected to this constant state of change and renewal.

The transmission of knowledge cannot be separated from manipulation. First one must let go again of all the learned ideas in order to be able to develop an eye for the character of things. Afterwards one can still be irritated by the form something takes on or in which something is depicted. 63)

The jargon of authenticity, however, united the heterogeneous under one roof. Linguistic components from an individual sphere – from theological tradition, existential philosophy, the youth movement, the military or from Expressionism – are institutionally absorbed and then, to a certain extent, returned to the private sphere, placed back in the possession of the individual person, who can then speak with ease, freedom, and joy about mission and encounter, about authentic pronouncement and concern, as though he himself were pleased. In truth, he is only putting on airs, as though each individual were his own announcer on FM radio. 64)

It is assumed that the text works like a simulation of memory itself, where manifold elements flow together and are mounted onto a fragile construct of remembrances – an inextricable conglomeration of autobiographical facts, things seen on television, gathered from conversations, read, and found in the various other media. Sometimes it is not clear where the border between individual experiences and external material lies. Memory fills up the empty spaces by combining, selecting, and arranging moments of reality in the present, which then obtain sense, validation, positioning, and integration in the system by creating associative patterns from what has already been experienced in the past.

Mistaken sorting happens frequently, to the absurd degree that plots of books and movies become unconsciously integrated into personal experiences in order for the person to achieve personal continuity. Like a montage, these parts are absorbed and become so indistinguishable from the autobiographic parts that they seem real. Established neurological patterns are flexible and are exposed to a continuous review and update of the individual connections within the pattern as a whole. Actual experiences and emotions in the present define the existing pattern anew in an interplay between memory and the perception of the external material: authenticity and truth are difficult and no longer reliable concepts and of secondary importance for brain activity.

All underlined parts in the text indicate citations from diverse heterogeneous sources, which most often are taken out of context but which nonetheless support, back up, and enhance the principal text in a non-scientifically based dimensionality. At the same time, the author's personal commentary is broken up, fragmented, and interwoven with external opinions. The assessment consists in the quotation itself. These citations are often translations (occasionally, but rarely unofficial); however, the possible slight changes of meaning sporadically engendered as a result of the translations can be interesting. Fuzziness at the author's discretion is probable and possible, and he believes that a citation should ideally be released at the moment it is written down or spoken and be freely available within a cultural field for further processing. This standpoint is in accordance with the idea of open source in terms of supporting a democratic, general access to knowledge and information.

Such an intuitively superficial way of dealing with citations and texts on no account shows ignorance or disrespect to the writers involved, but results from a simulation of the functionalities of perception itself. For the specific purposes of the experiment and the applied method, an authorised and verified referencing is neither mandatory nor necessary when focussing on the observation of the act of processing – with all the possible losses and changes that could ensue – instead of wishing for absolute exactness of content or an objectivity in the theses, both of which are untenable. How the reader deals with the presented material and his or her conscious or unconscious enrichment of it with personal content (defining meaning) indicates the outlines and central subject of the examination. In this regard every sort of content can be integrated into the discourse, including content that is worthless in a scientific sense, because a priori worthless content does not exist.

Ideally a book would have no order to it and the reader would have to discover his own. 60)

The possibility for self-expression lies in the arrangement of the finished parts as soon as the psychological dimension of the one who is doing the arranging has been included. 61)

The formal methods of displaying texts are montage, assemblage, combination, reproduction, and copying, as ways of putting all of the information on the same two-dimensional plane. Through repeated use, set pieces become symbols. Analogous to how visual material is treated, pieces of text are combined, become redundant; are borrowed, found, and reused; extracted from the original frame of reference, transformed, absorbed, and deepened; influenced and suffused with different and eventually differing viewpoints; and present themselves as metalayers.

As with life itself, the topics are not prescribed: the intuitive, misunderstood, and incomprehensible, scientific, pseudo-scientific, or miscarried, trivial or popular, intellectual, not reflected upon, and kitsch all compete with one another and obtain more than a simple consensus, a demonstration of power through a definite and predominant opinion, or the mediocrity of a common denominator. Our own personal views change nearly imperceptibly, a little each day, and have to be constantly revised because of new realisations. Behaviour patterns alter according to the social context in which they are expressed.

The accompanying theoretical texts correspond to the images in propounding a fragmental, contradictory, multi-dimensional, and incoherent bricolage appropriated from heterogeneous sources: single blocks of text stand alone and nevertheless relate to others because of the spatial or formal proximity between them – contrasting, contradicting, or intensifying each other, or even formulating additional ideas and concepts. From the physical viewpoint the density of the material all seems the same at first glance. The viewer's perception decides through selection if any, and if so which, value is assigned to something. In the opinion of physicist Werner Heisenberg, nothing can be examined without the examiner's being changed by doing so. Although it is impossible to maintain a completely neutral position because making a selection and cataloguing it already represents a valuation of the material, nevertheless an attempt has been made to try to maintain a certain distance from the material in order to grant the reader the greatest possible freedom to accept or reject it. The sources are manifold: some are literal citations, some just the gist of information stored somewhere in the back of this author's head, and some picked up in public places. They can speak for themselves and will hopefully generate discourses establishing new relationships. If these findings are already well known, the viewer can agree with them because of a feeling that in the visuals, something has been expressed and brought up that he or she already knew.

The numbering of the pages runs in reverse order, from back to front, in order to support and intensify the impression of the non-linear without completely giving up a marginal frame of reference. Texts are turned at a 90-degree angle to disengage the direction for reading and viewing from its formal restraints without sacrificing legibility. The book is stripped bare to the essentials, and devoid of a protecting cover.

The theoretical background of this book is as trivial as the thoughts of any given person. Most are common and well-known approaches from various sources, reproduced and reconsidered before being restated in this context and then adapted to suit the concept. Originality and authorship are outdated: no one person's work can be viewed in isolation, the only possible form of originality being *authentic forgery* (Luc Tuymans). A text manifests itself as a product of fragments of what has been read and reread, has evolved, been reinterpreted, heard, casually picked up, or misinterpreted. According to Roland Barthes everything is a citation and everything has already been said. Every text is an entanglement of quotations. The act of reproduction and repeated transcription between different media (copy and paste) has become an important cultural technique for disseminating information. Individuality is dismissed in an inextricable amount of citations comparable to the manifold narrative threads in the books of Thomas Pynchon or to the concept of hypertext: from literature to science, from sound to politics, from Lasse Marhaug to Noam Chomsky, from Niklas Luhmann to Important Records, and on to snatches picked up from telephone conversations in the underground. The extension of the research into various artistic and scientific fields enhances the amount of things one does not know exponentially. Everything becomes both complicated and easier, all at the same time. Getting lost eventually reveals itself to be a frightening, but relief-filled experience.

The consequence of the bold changes caused and accompanied by the fast-paced information technology is that perception apparently changes: the requirements shift from the capability to memorise and store information to a flexible concept of connectivity. Perhaps the skills of being able to compare contents and find unusual connections, relationships, and links will in the long term replace the main function of our brain as a medium for storing knowledge, with the result that copyrights and intellectual property will have to be reviewed and probably replaced by open source

59)
Jean Baudrillard: *Simulations*

It is in effect the medium – the very style of montage, of decoupage, of interpolation, solicitation, summation, by the medium – which controls the process of meaning. 59)

How far can the modularity of letters or symbols be dissolved and still be understandable? How does the information change? Is it possible to determine the transition between the sign-like and the object-like? Does the sign-like keep its abstract character in a real context? What happens with real objects when they are shown in an abstract context? Does text remain sign-like and abstract in competition with visual material? How does the content of the text cooperate with the message at the visual level? Are these two different layers which can not be resolved? Does striking through a text change its meaning? Is it an act of elimination or one of exposure and a strange way of attracting attention?

The text here represents an intermediate state embedded in a system of relations and coordinates, taking shape and developing the existing, but not implanting new ideas. It has been consciously interspersed with breaks, dead ends, and fragments that offer a possibility to dock and connect. Contradictions correspond with the visual rules and are kept to challenge the recipient. Movable pieces of scenery counter what might seem to be static and authoritarian structures: the complementary lists of sources on the following pages are neither recommendations, nor are they essential for a deeper understanding, but represent an unrestricted invitation to grapple with the topic on a deeper level. They can be regarded as an open referential system that may either help or confuse

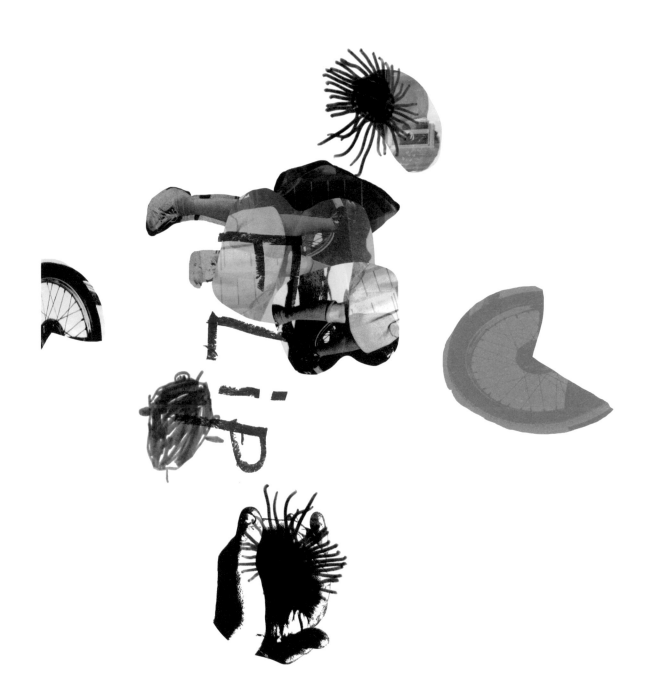

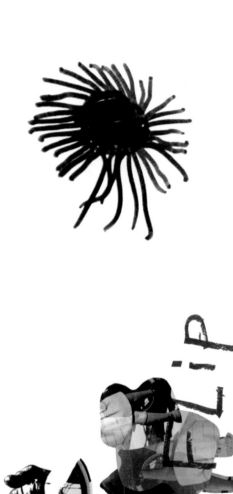
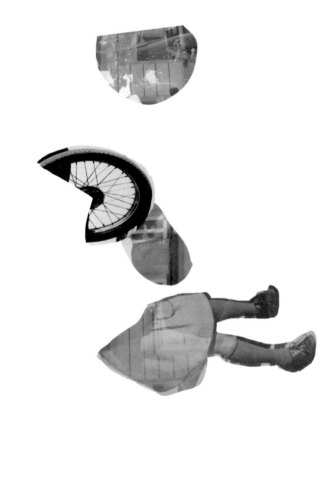

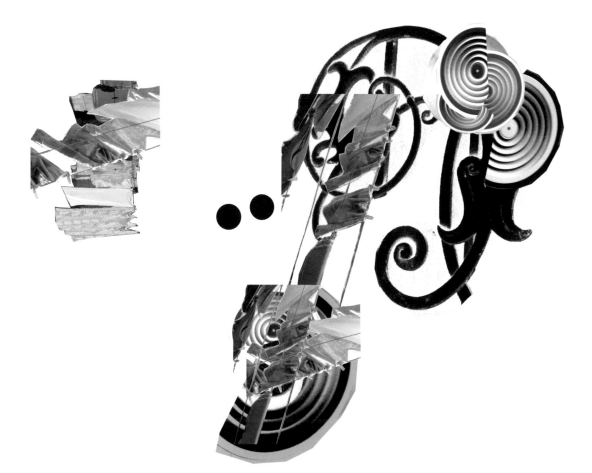

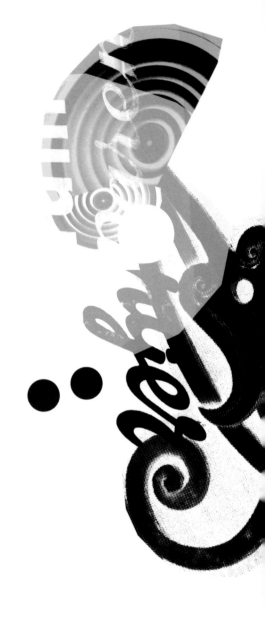
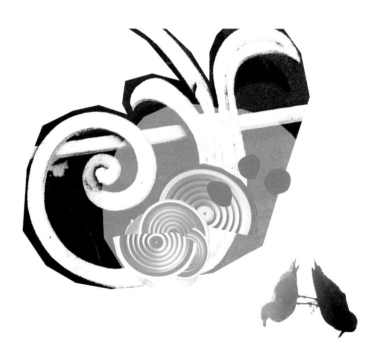

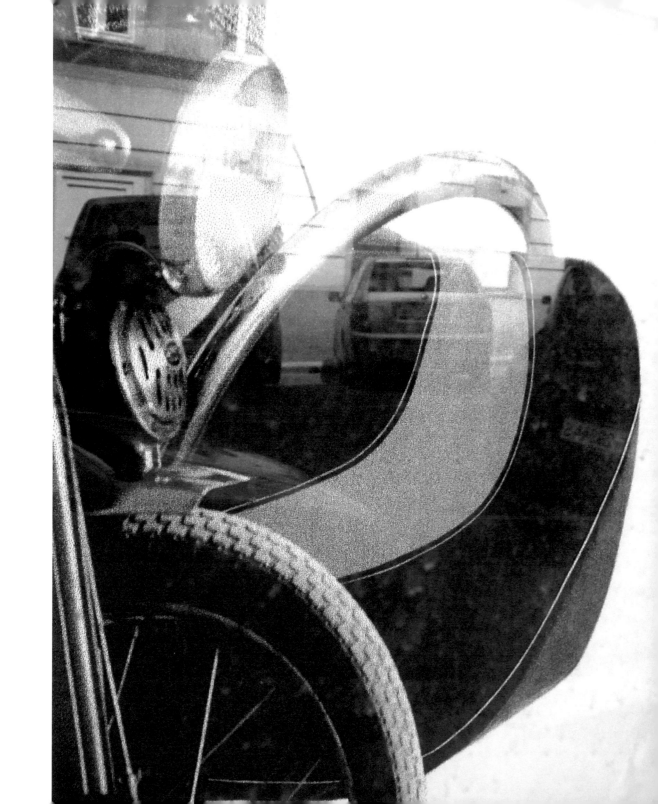

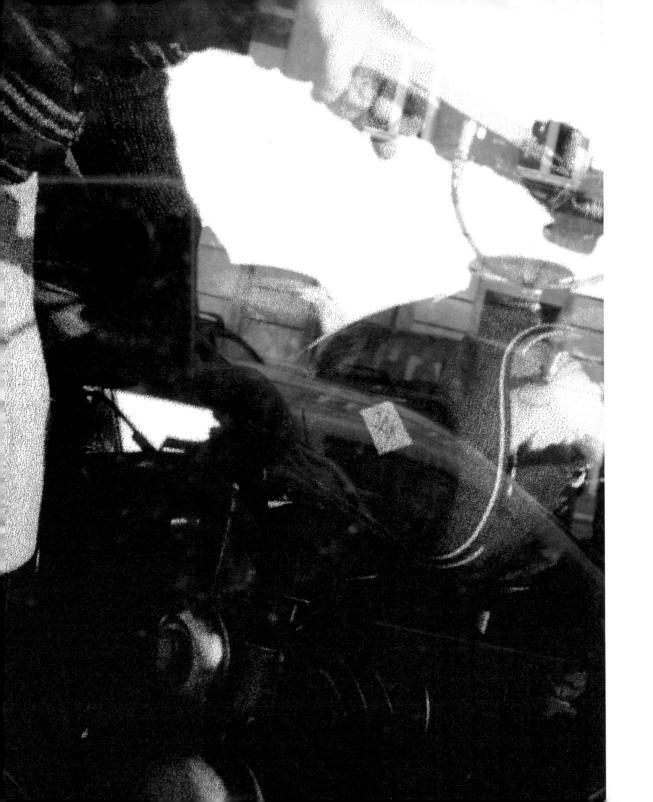

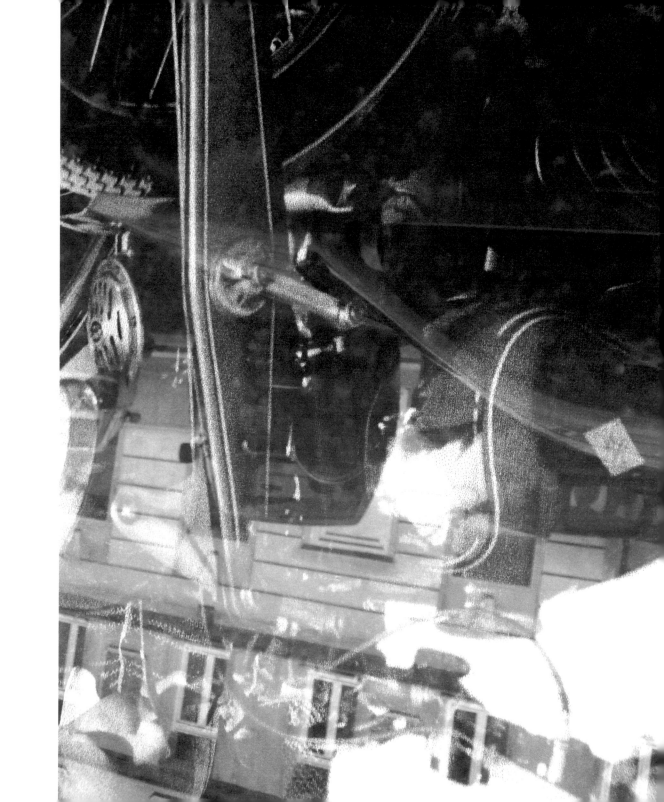

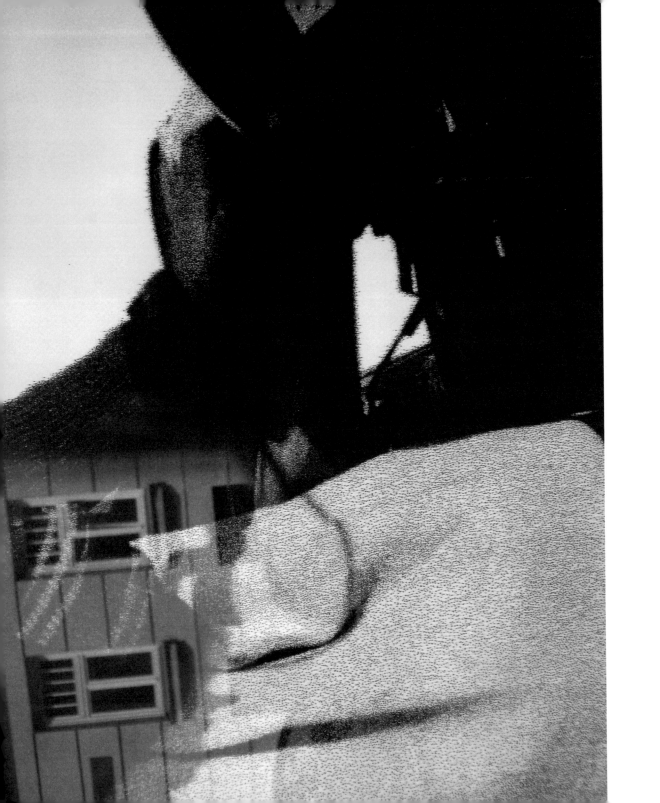

18/17

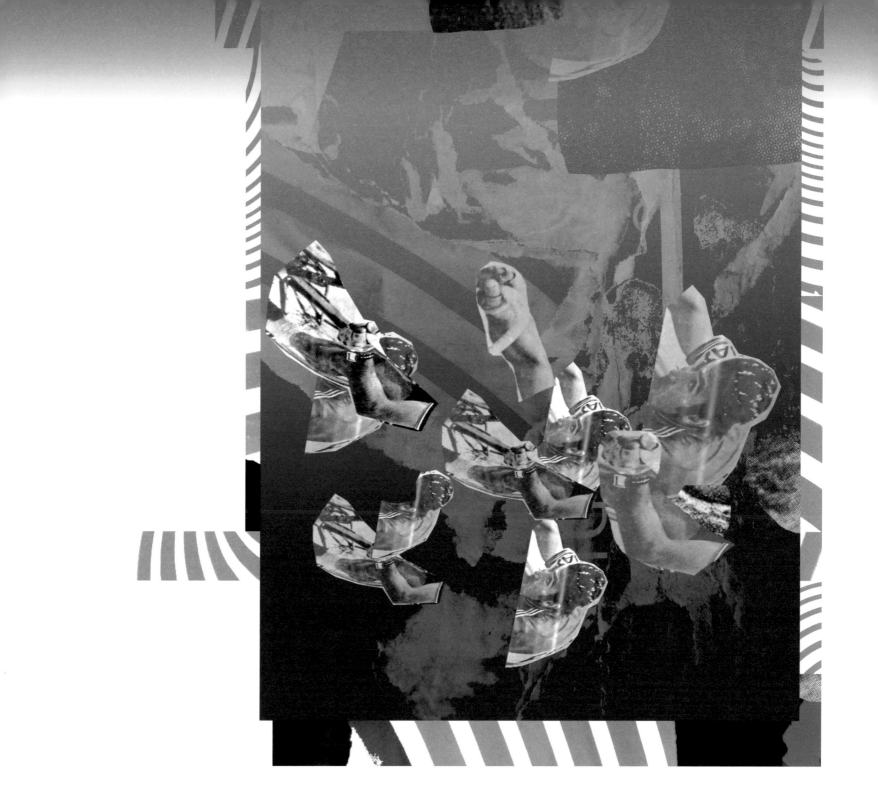

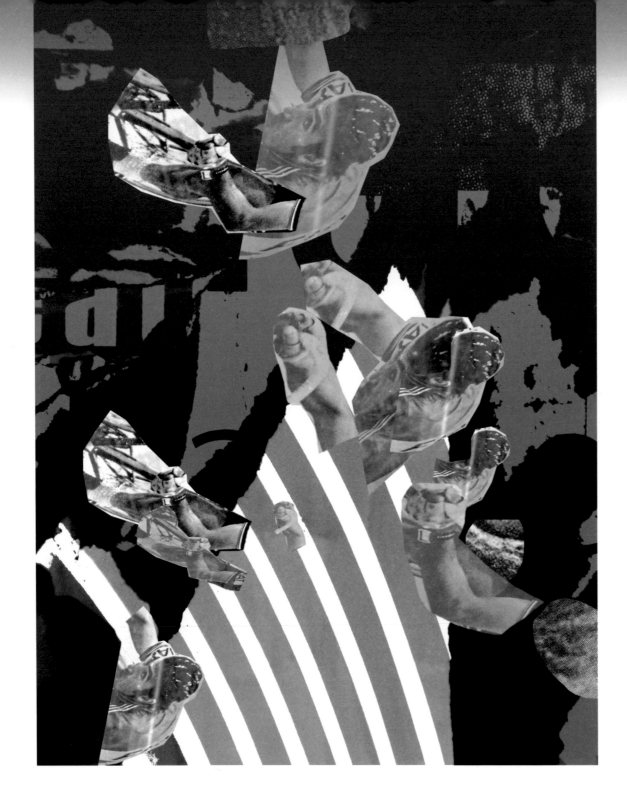

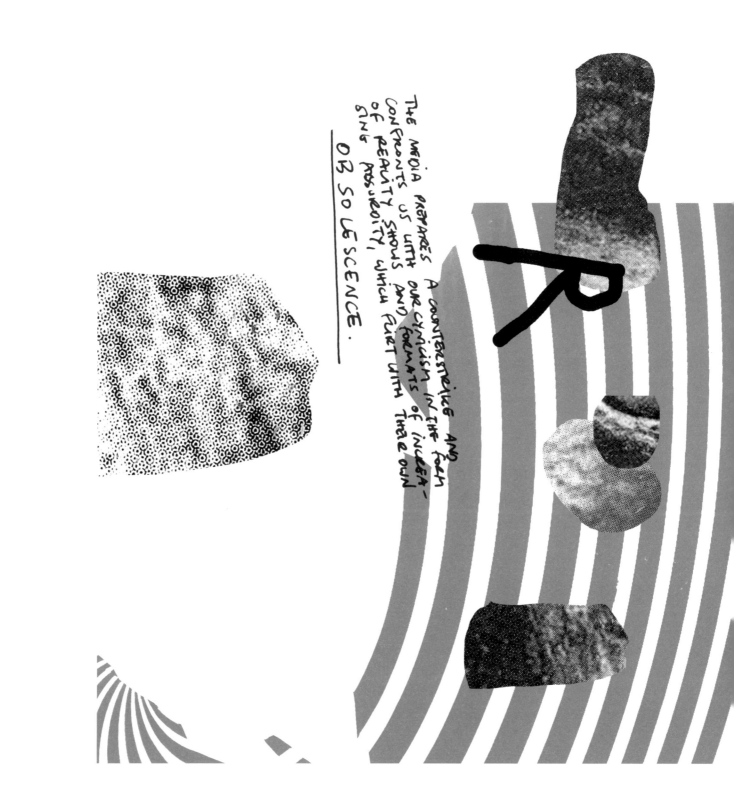

THE MEDIA PREPARES
CONFRONTS US WITH OUR CYNICISM IN THE FACH
OF REALITY SHOWS AND FORMATS OF INCREA-
STNG ABSURDITY, WHICH FLIRT WITH THEIR OWN

A COUNTERSTRIKE AND

OBSOLESCENCE.

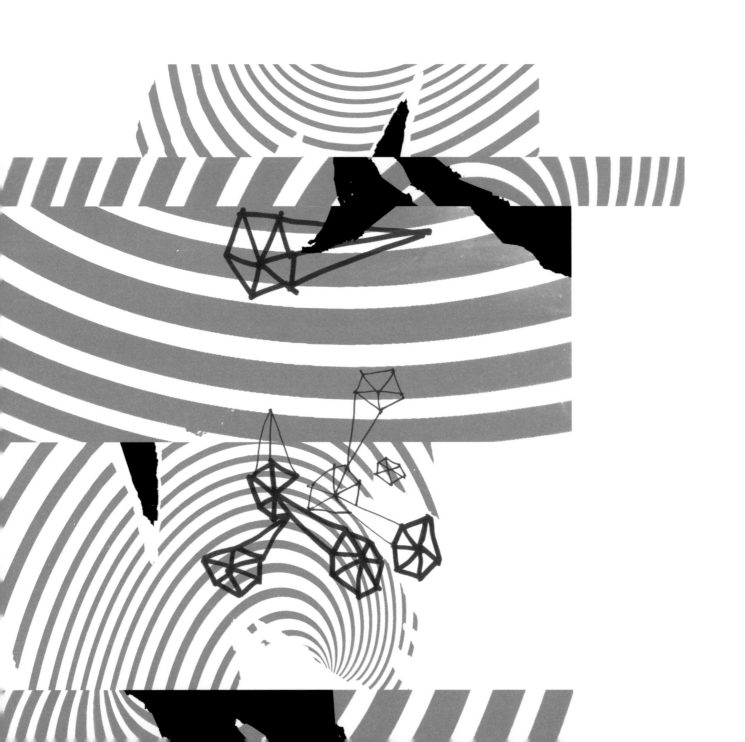

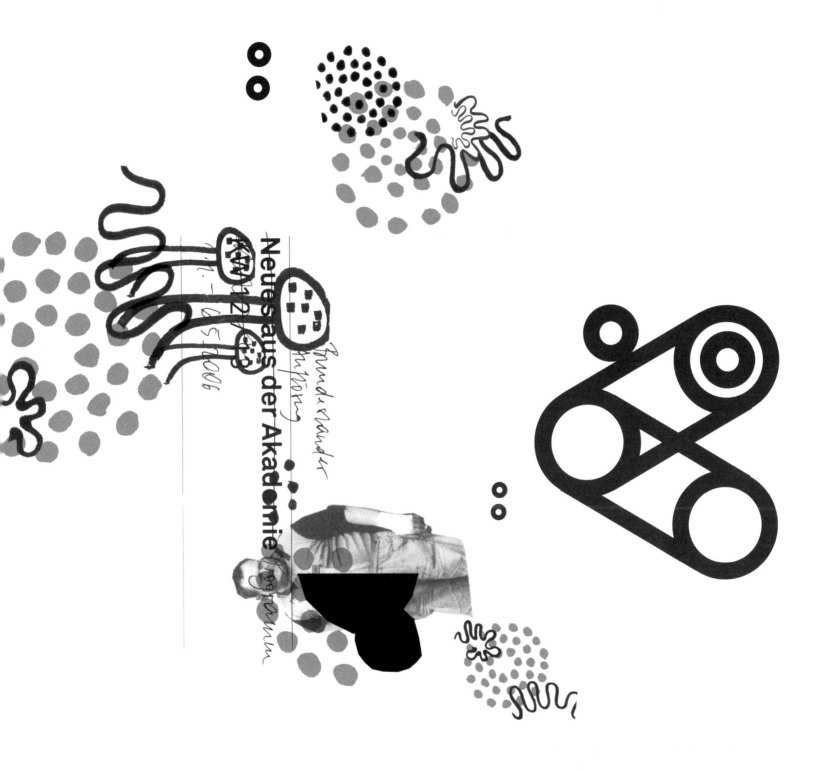

Neues aus der Akademie

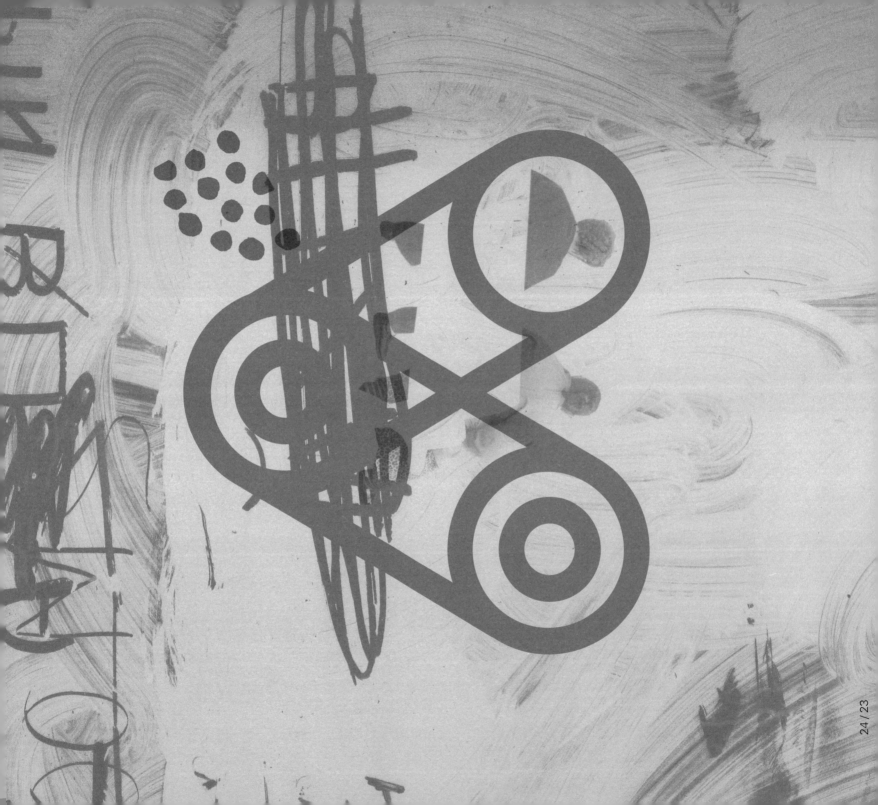

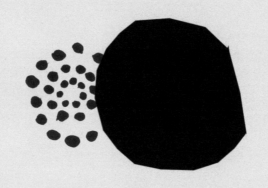

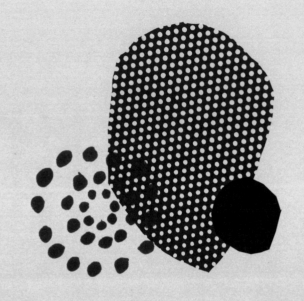

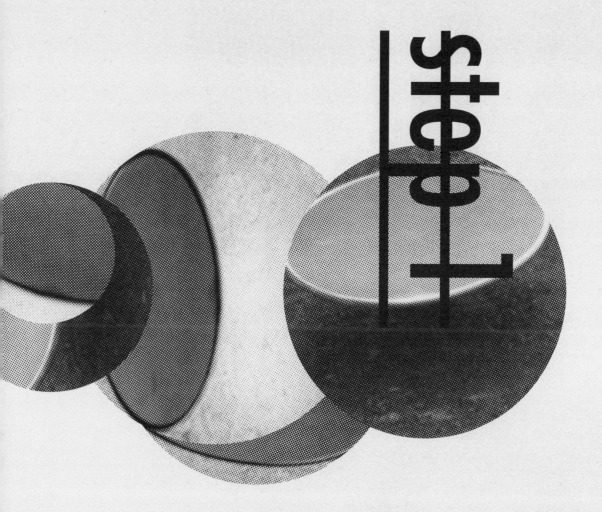

step 1

step 2

of 4

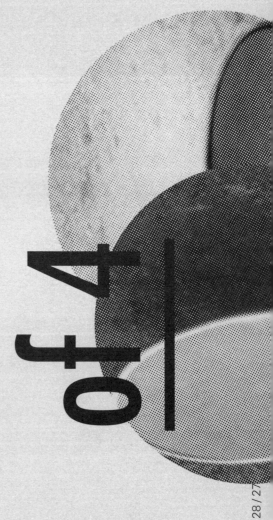

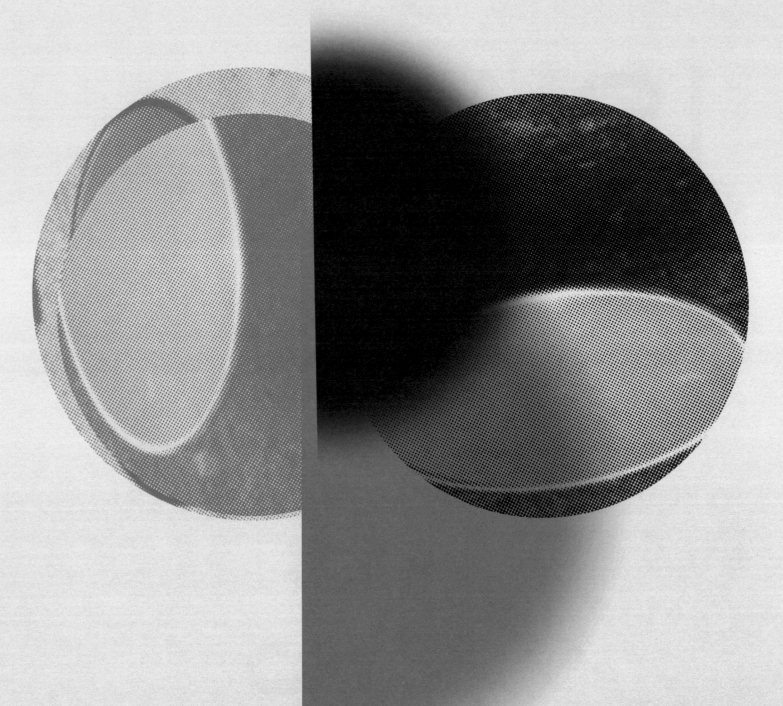

step 2

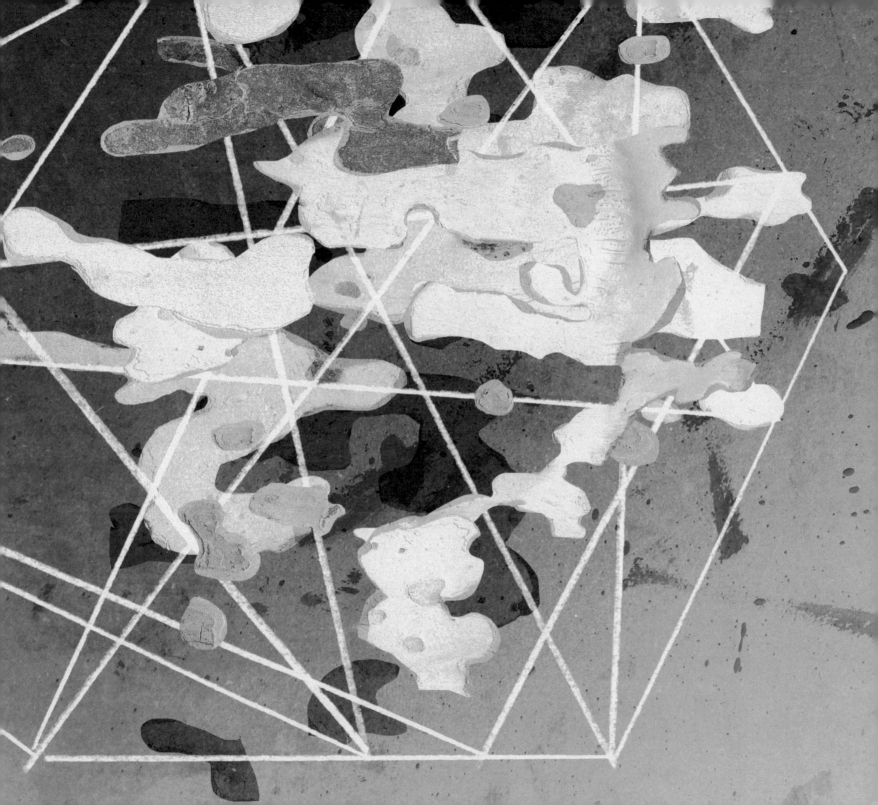

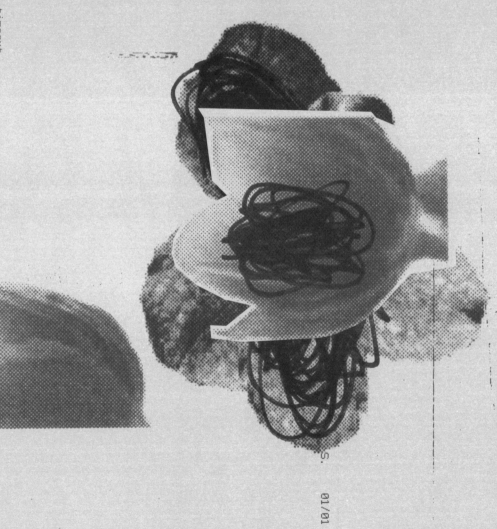

ERROR: timeout

24/03/2005 07:10

OFFENDING COMMAND: timeout

STACK:

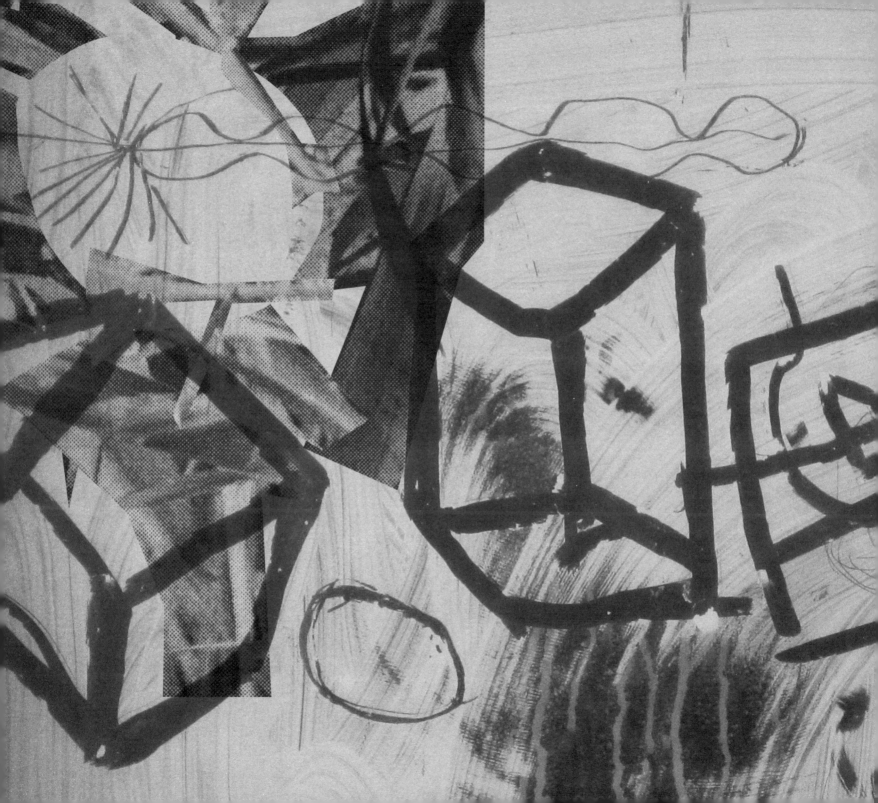

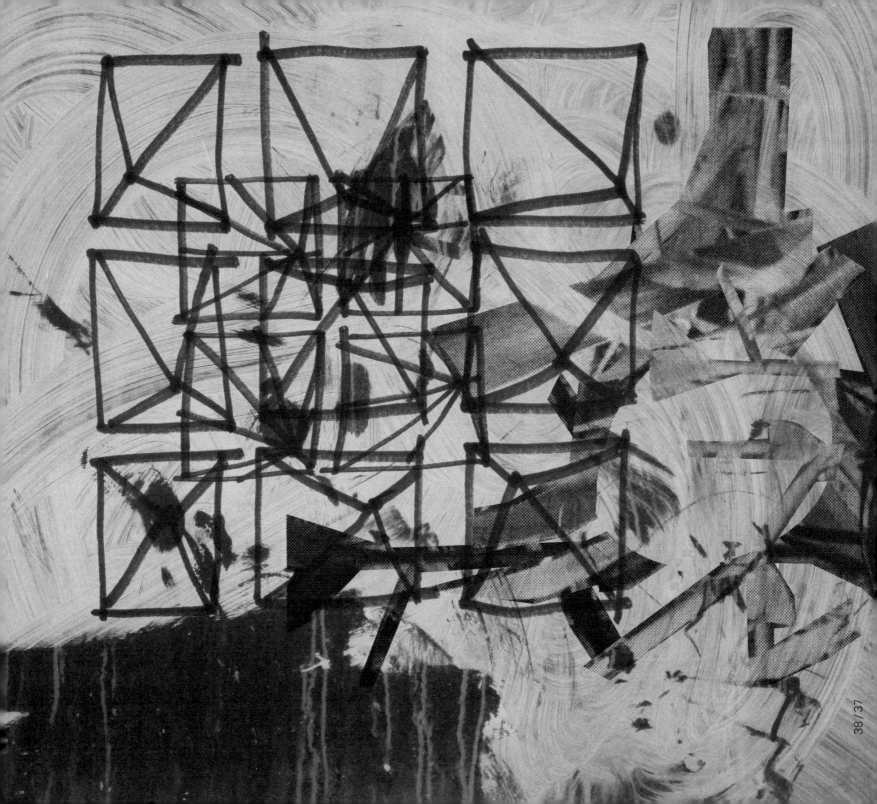

38/37

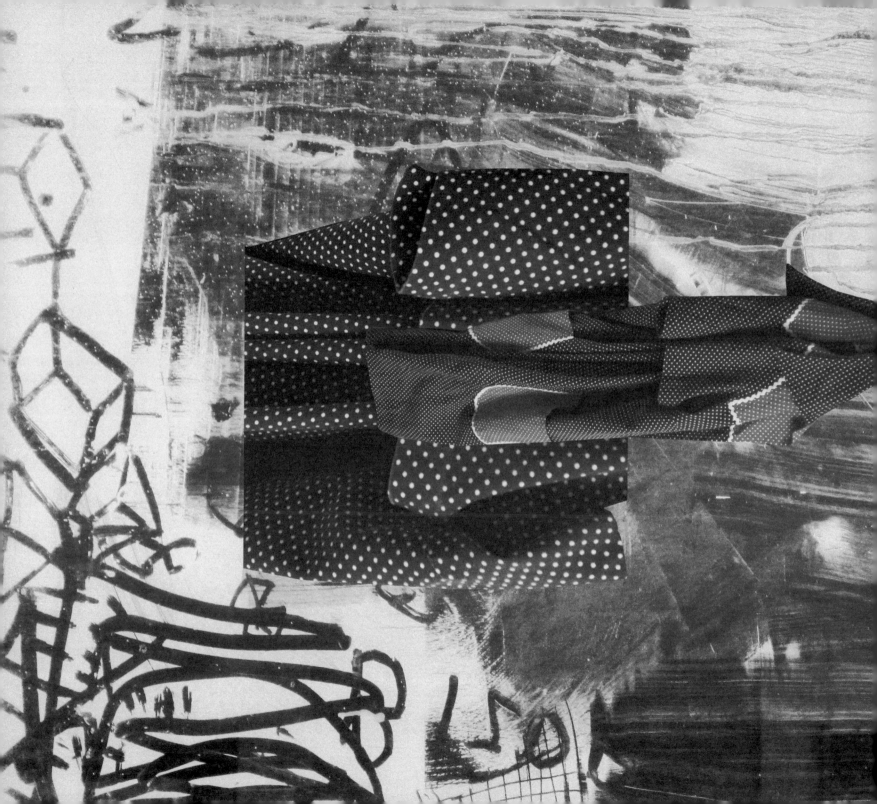

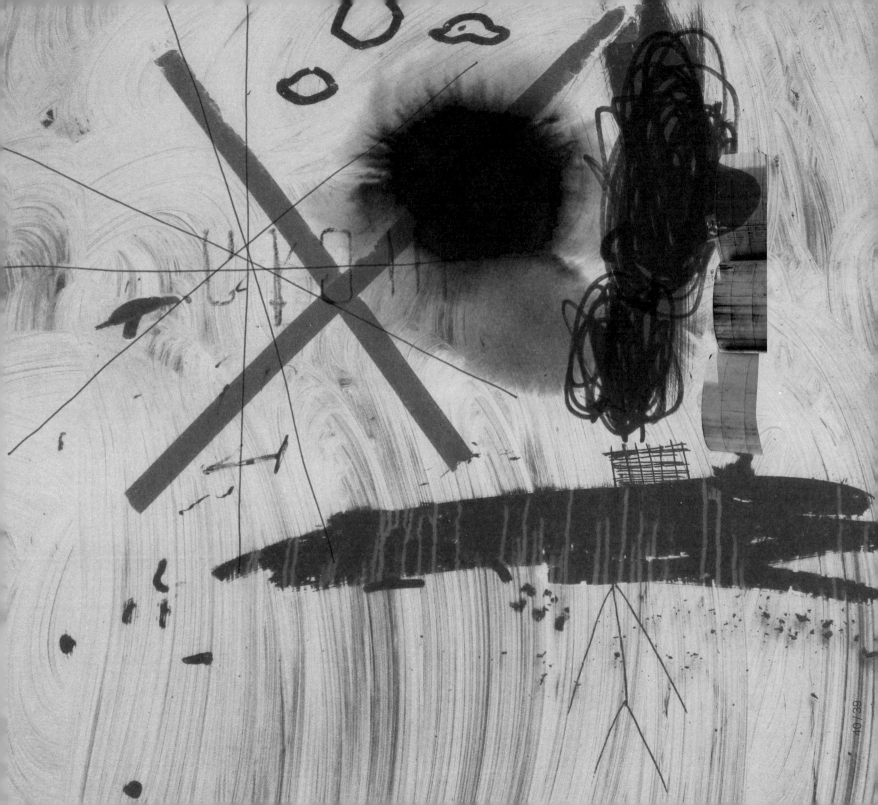

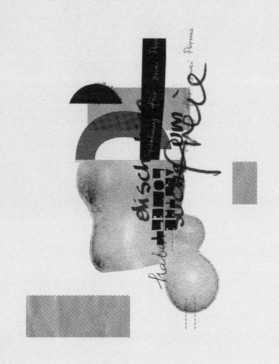

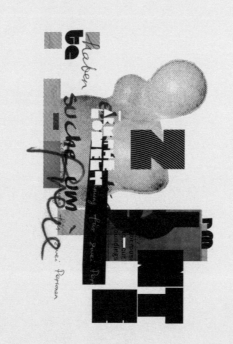

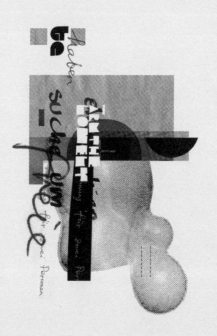

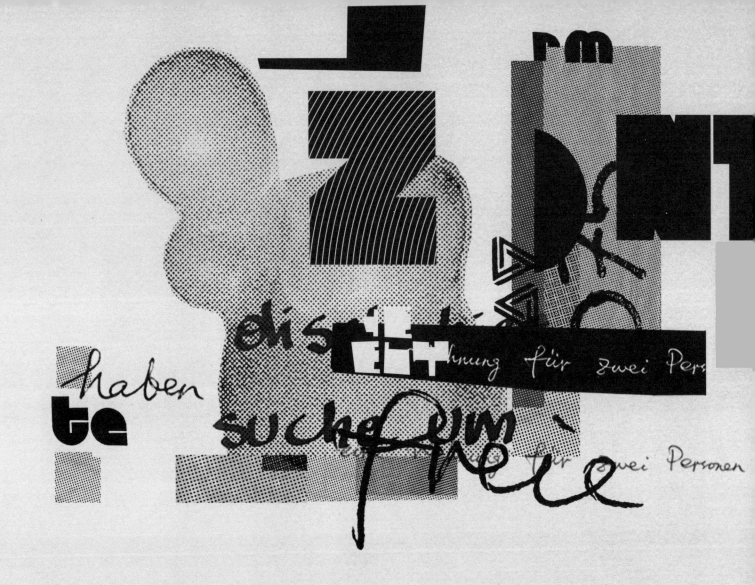

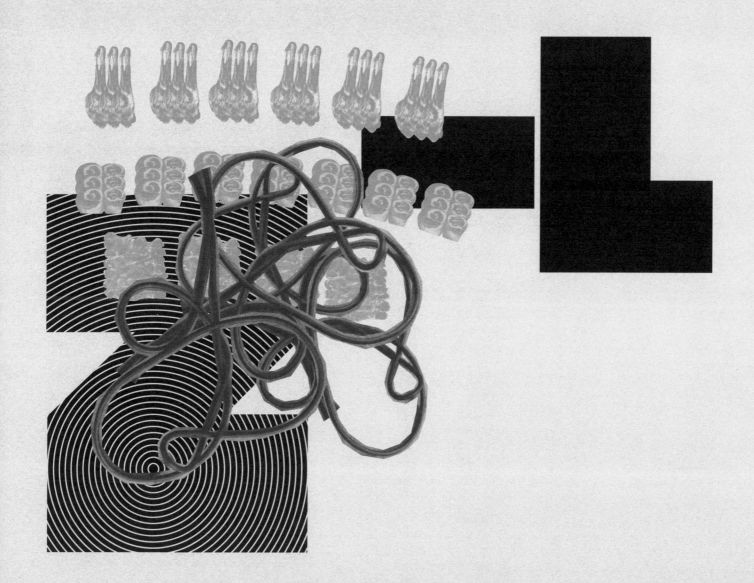

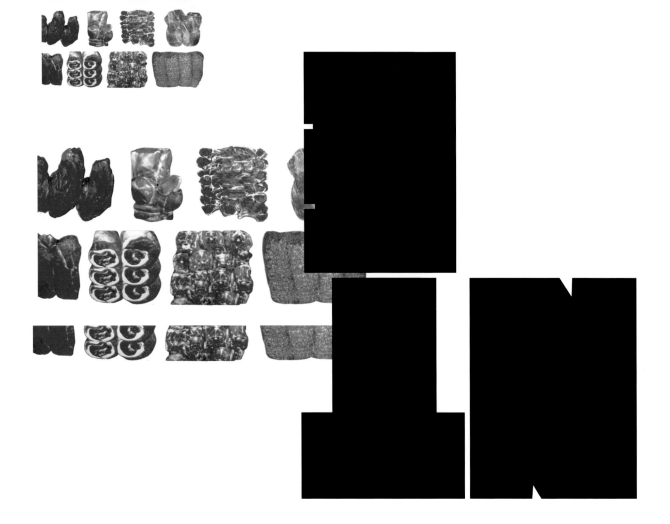

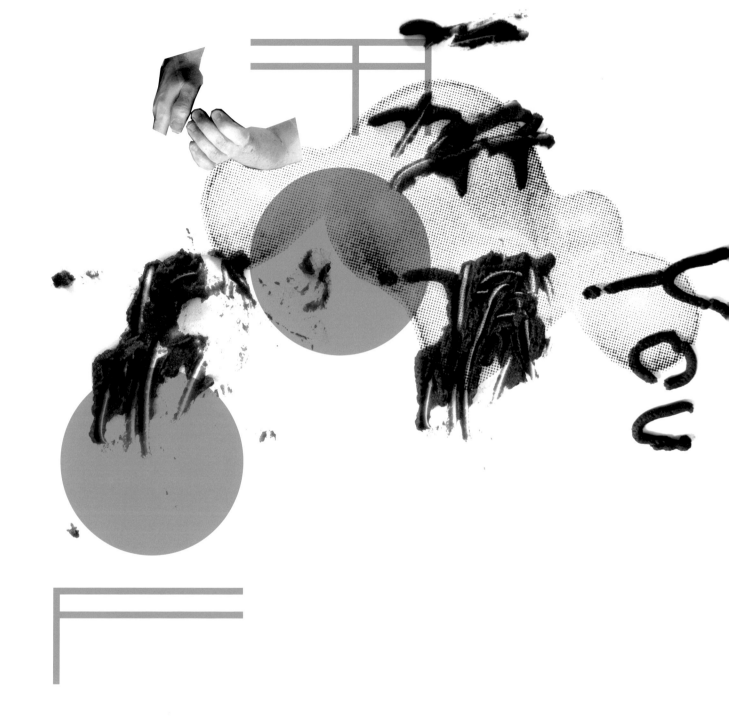

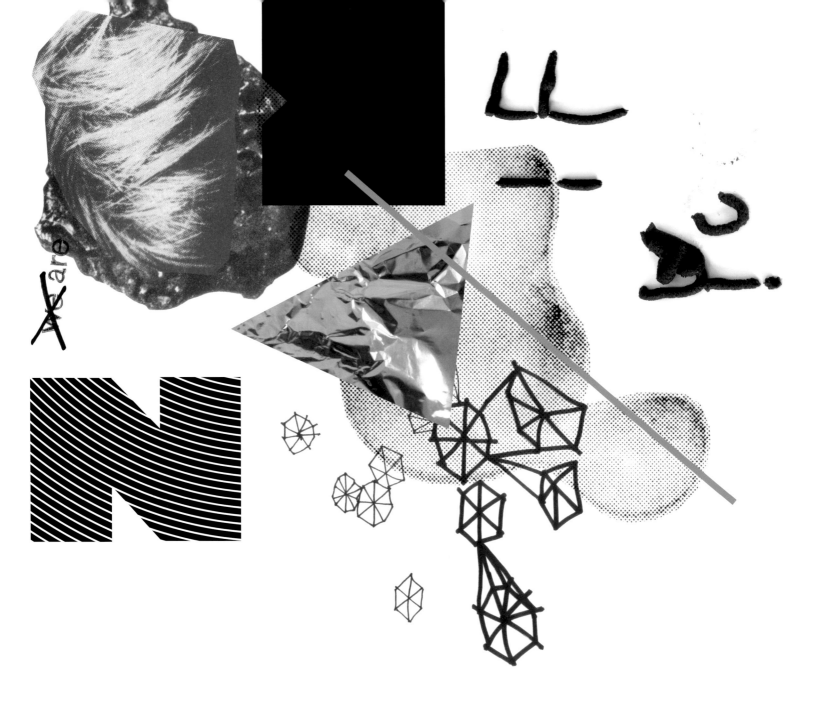

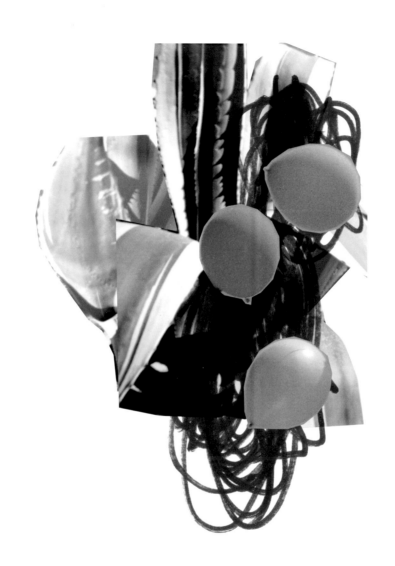

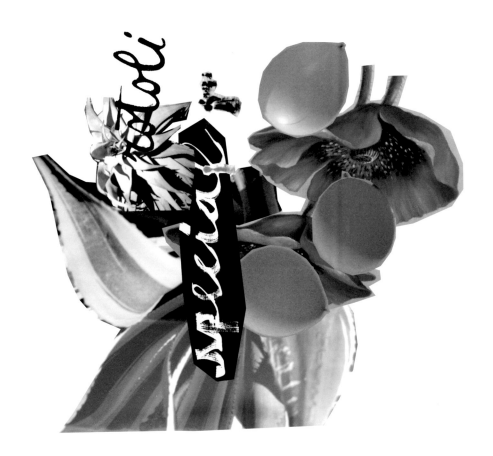

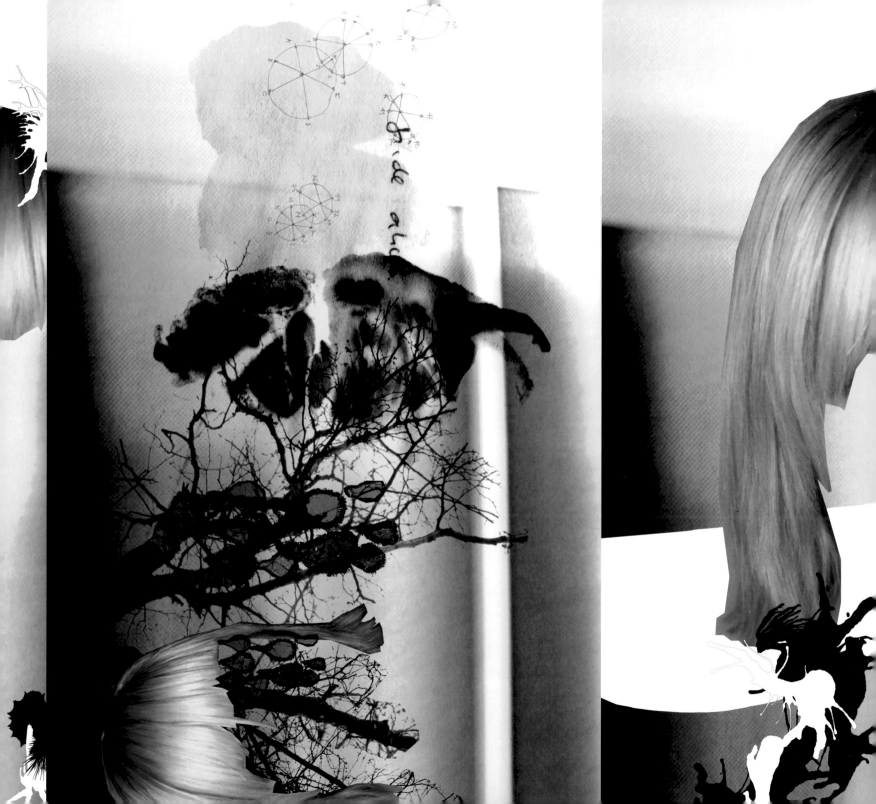

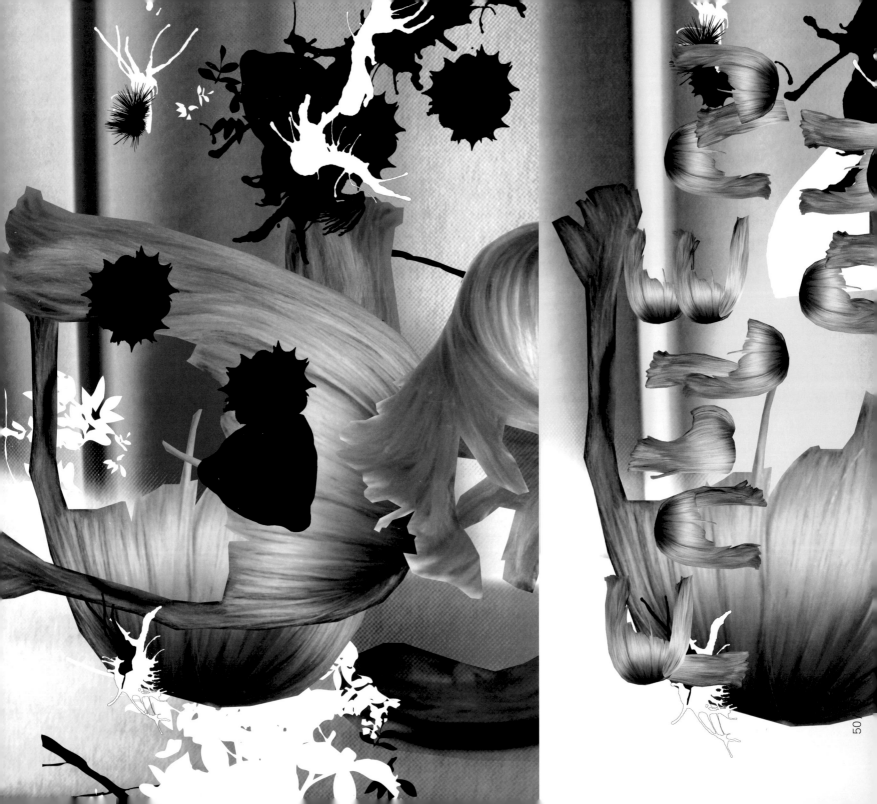

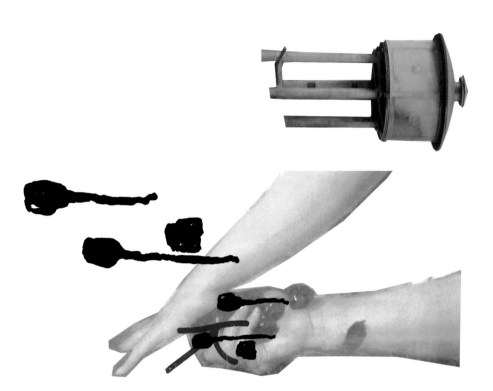

IF
THIS
IS ?
NOT
the
button is
nothing.

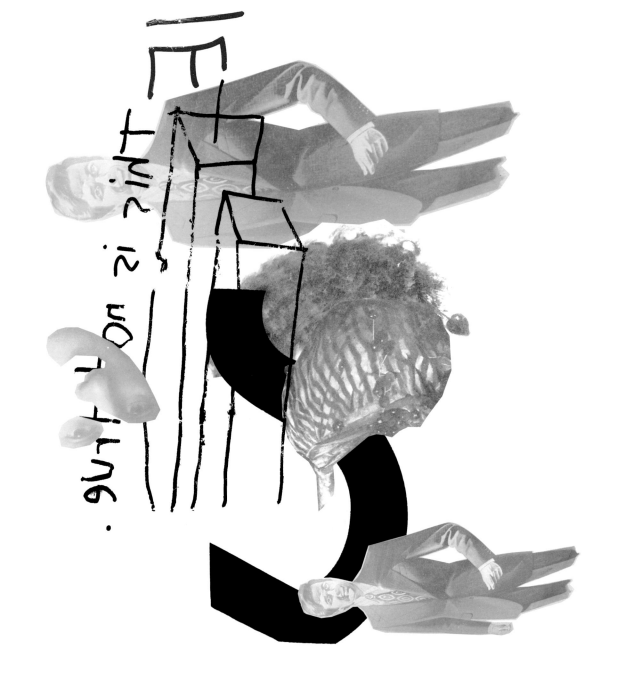

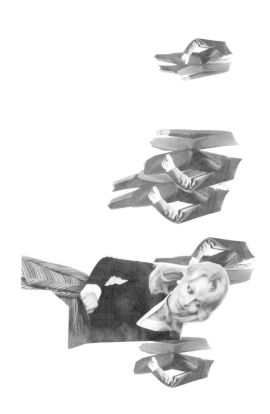
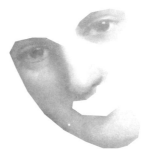

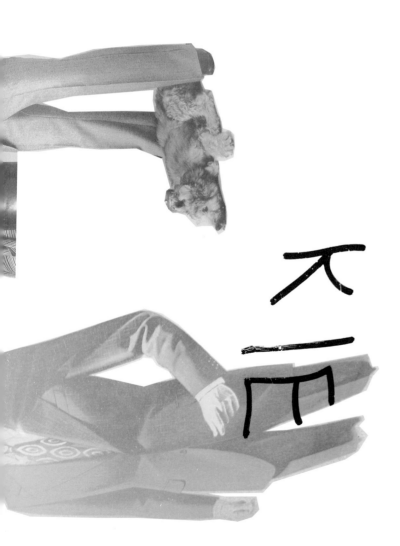

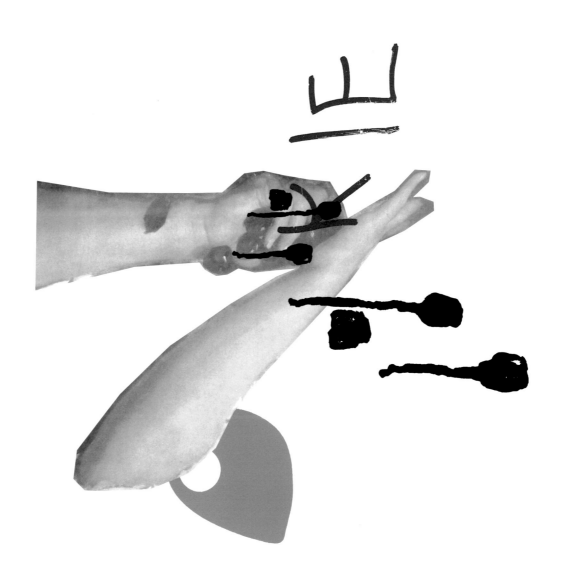

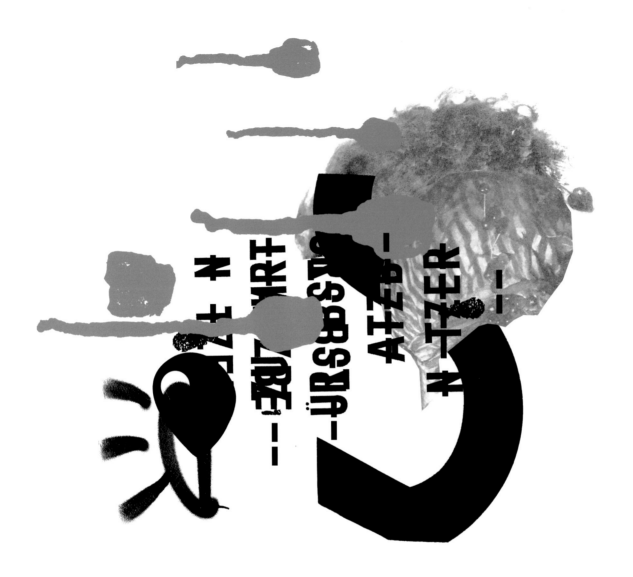

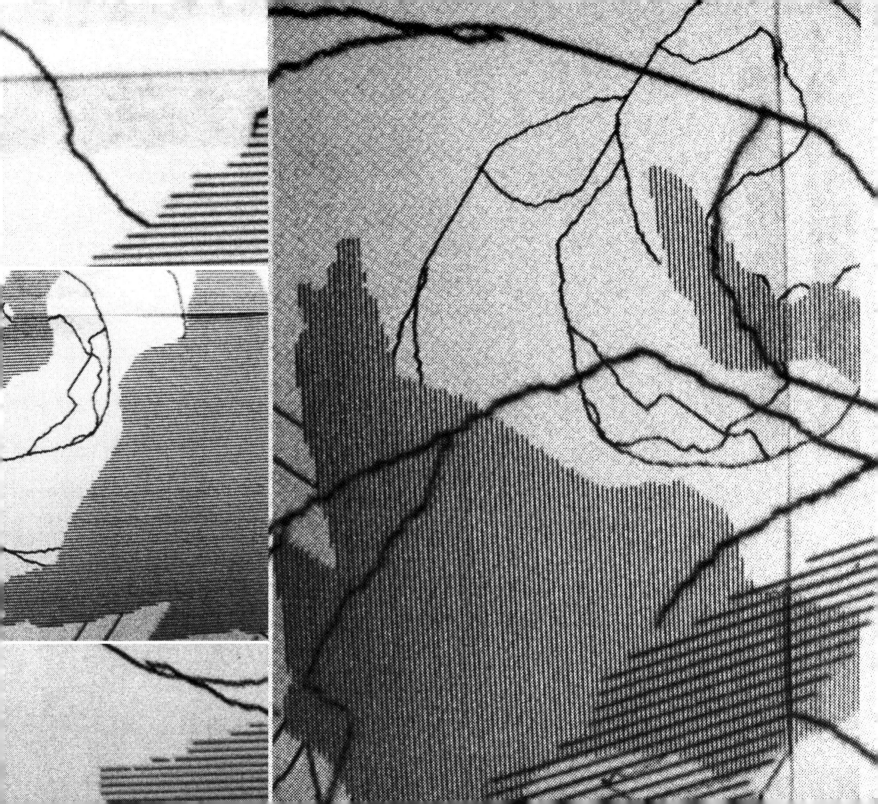

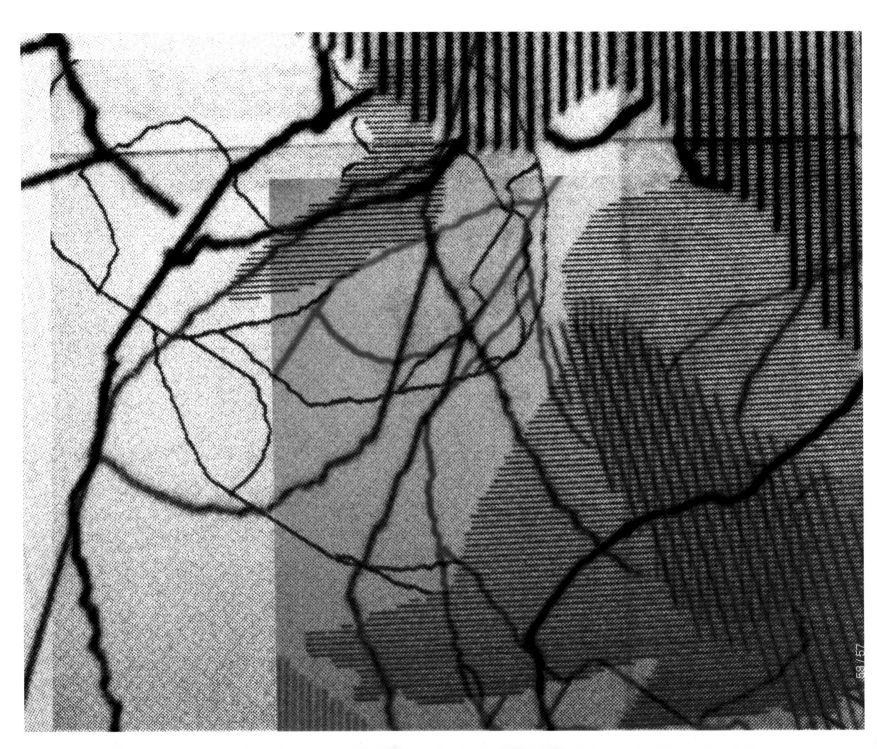

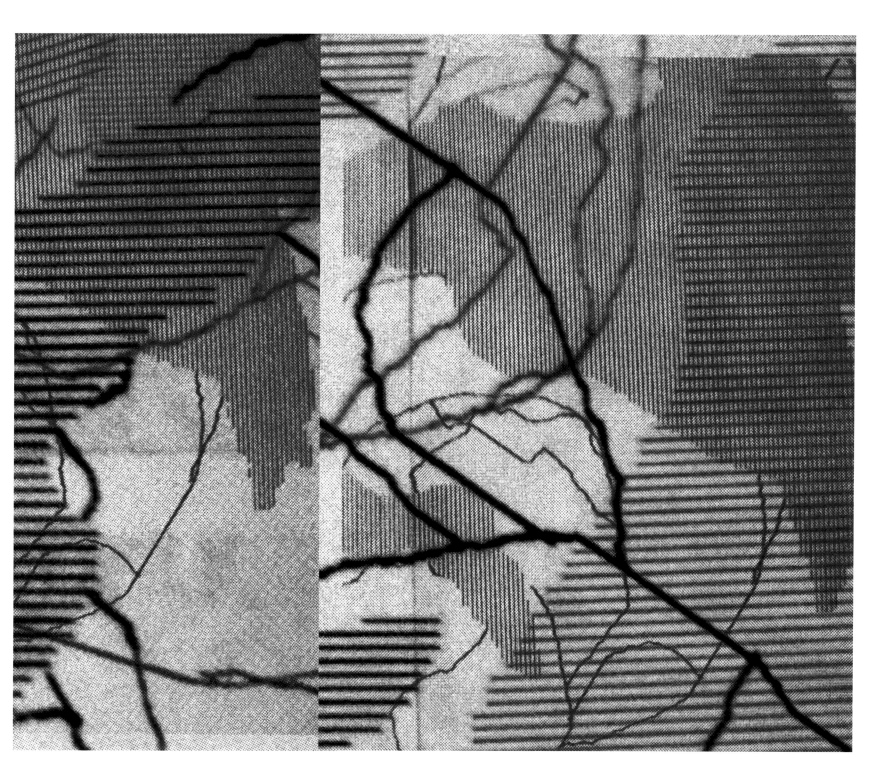

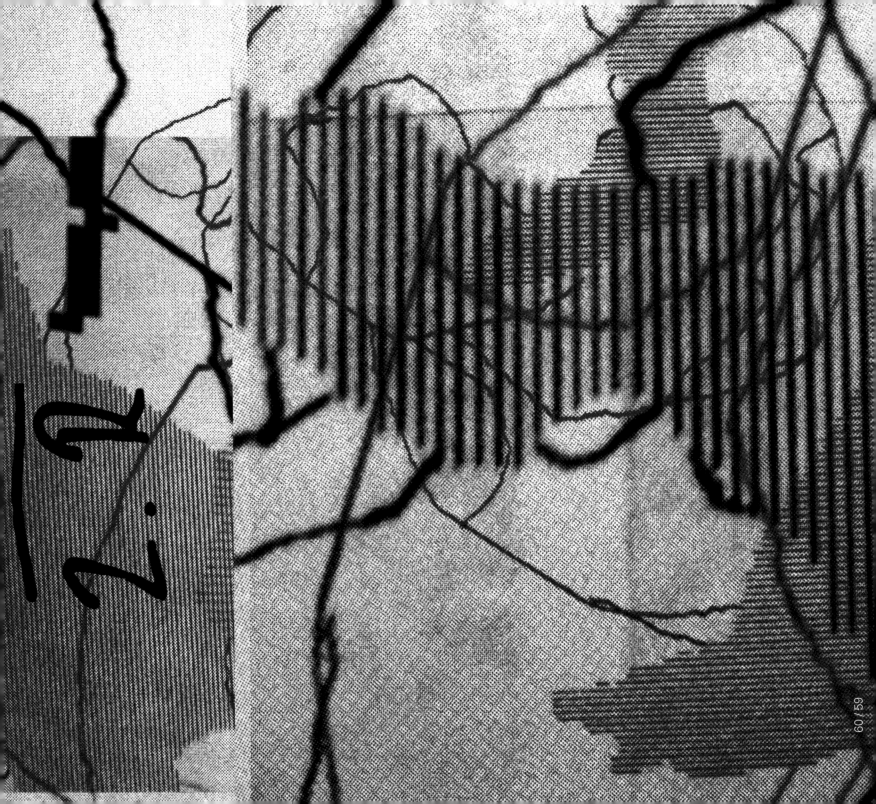

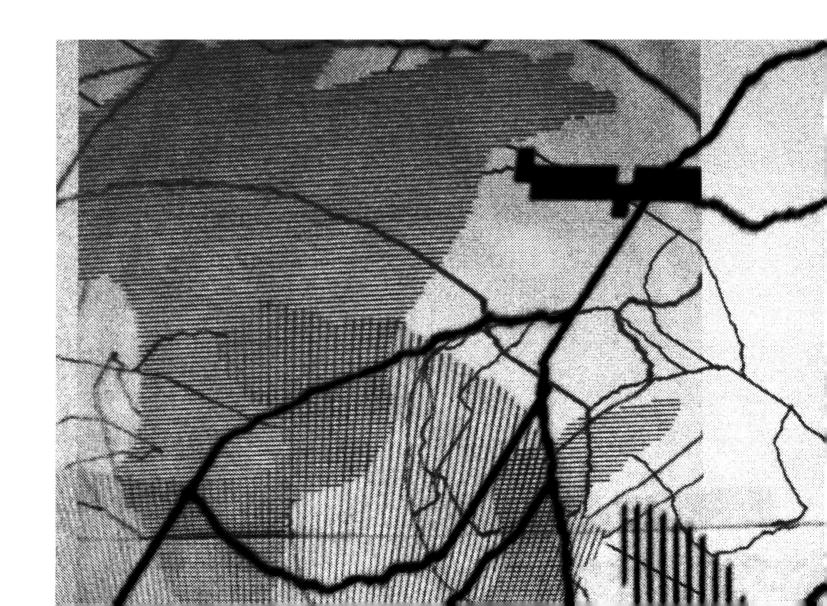

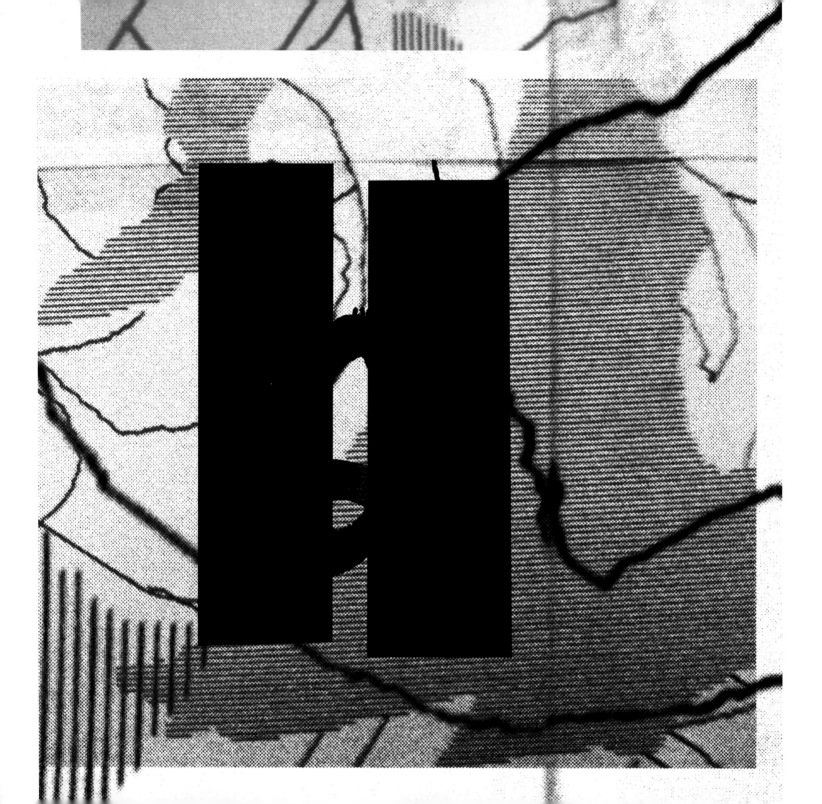

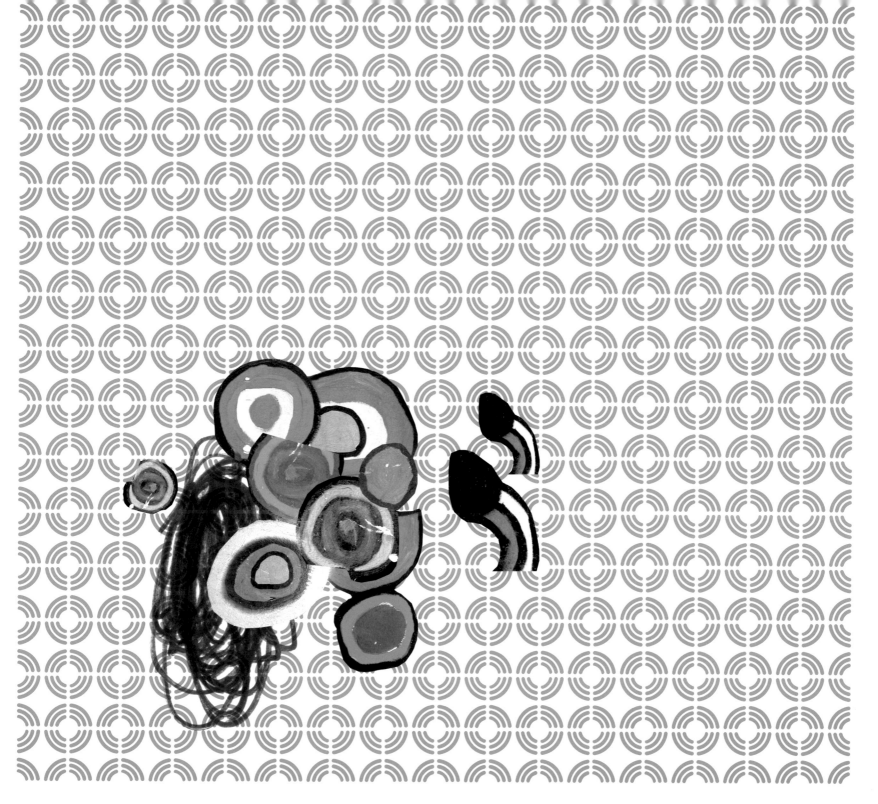

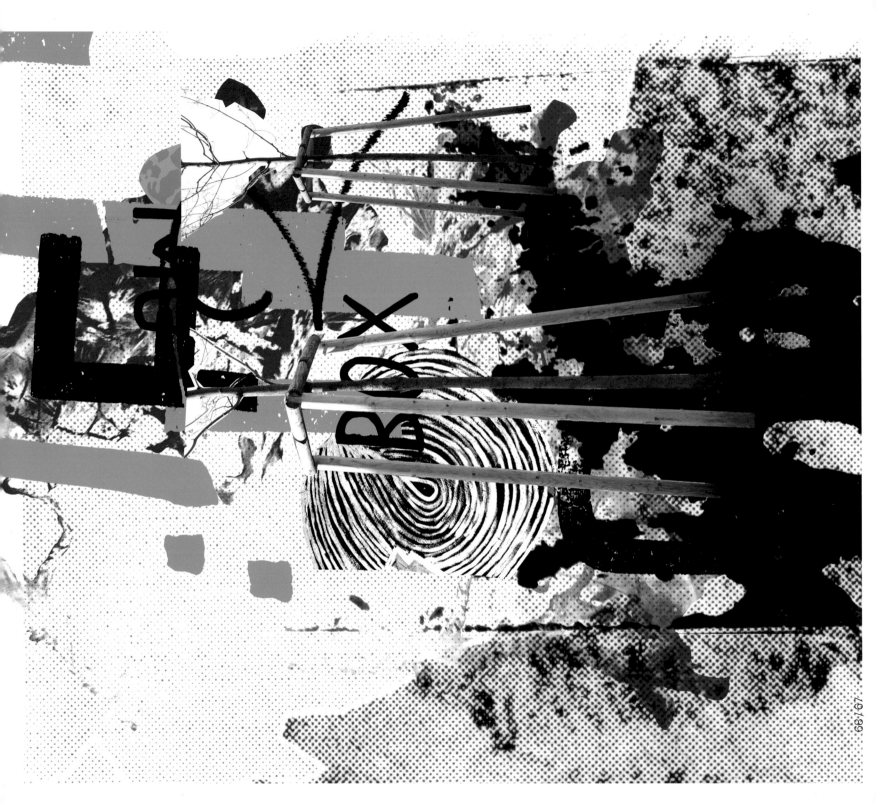

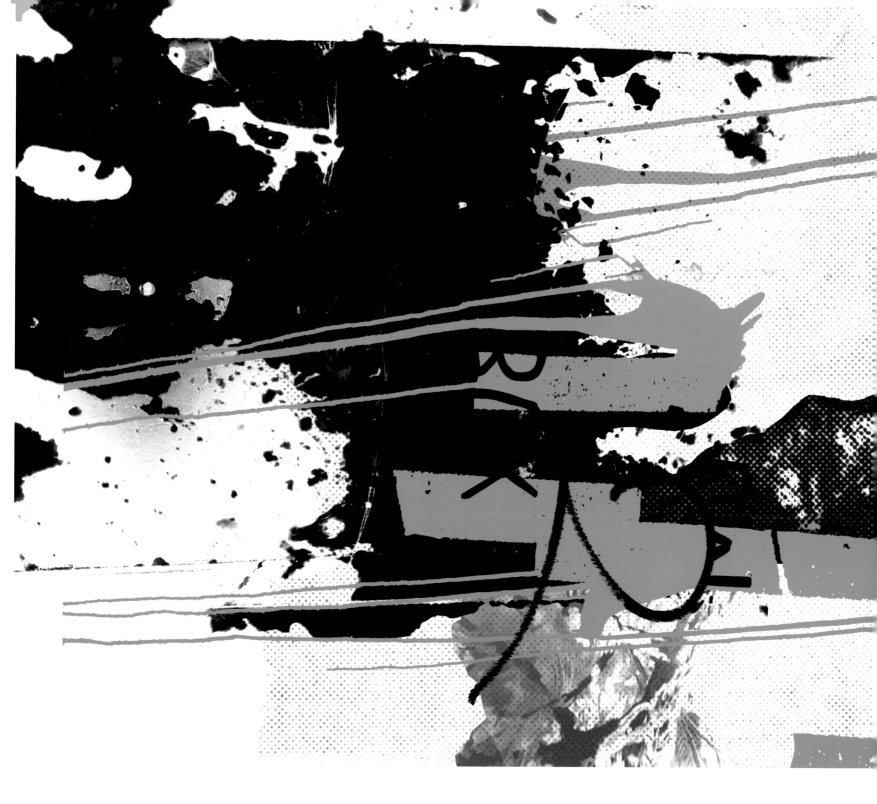

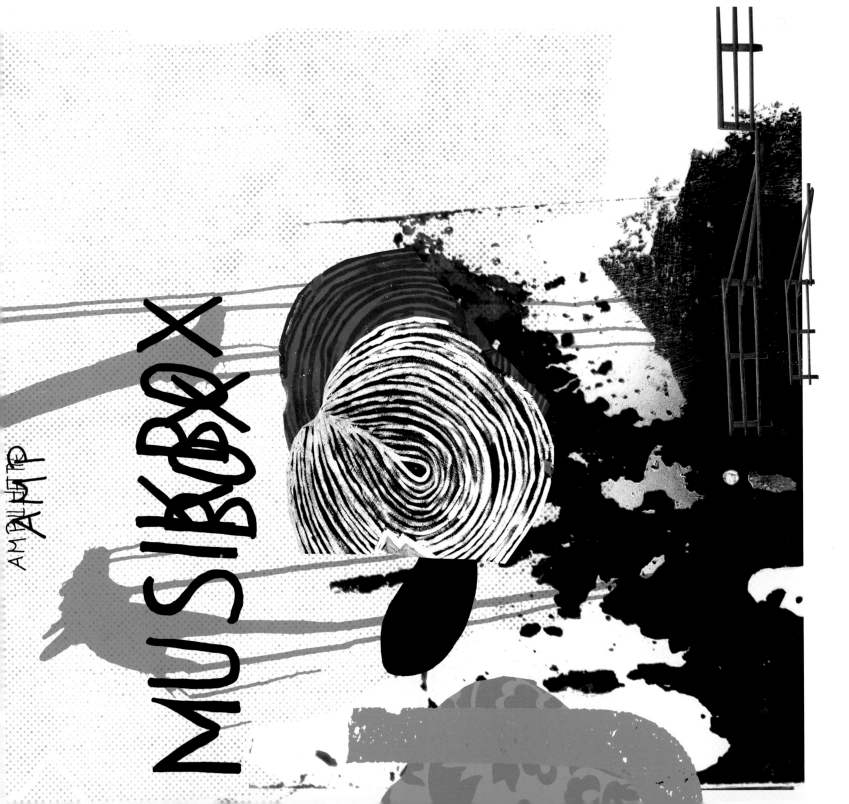

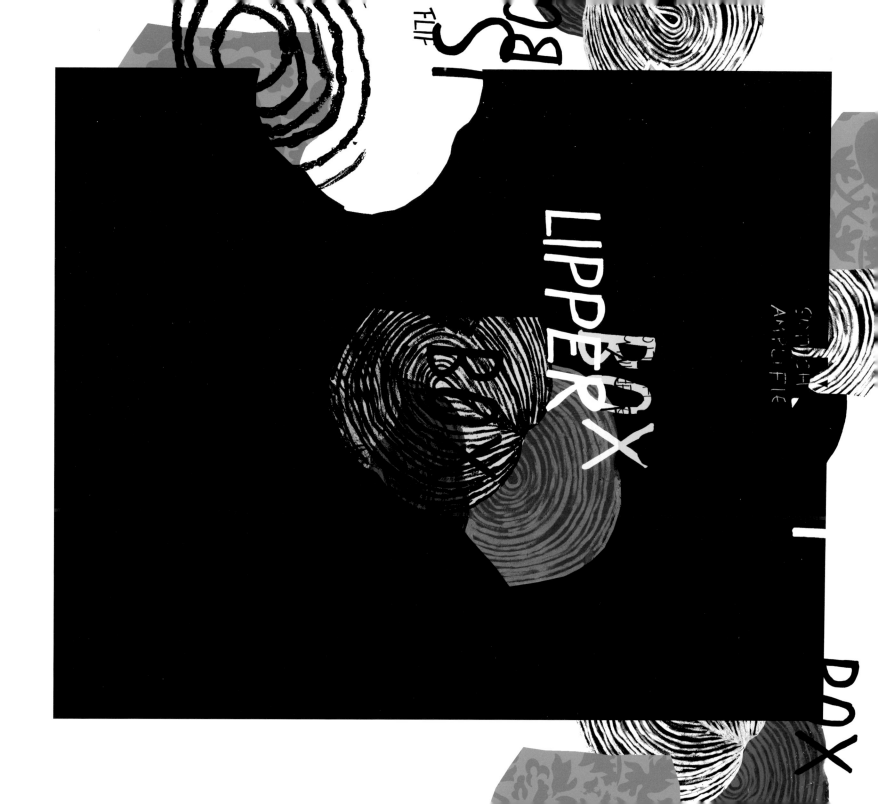

BOX

SWITCH
AMPAINTP

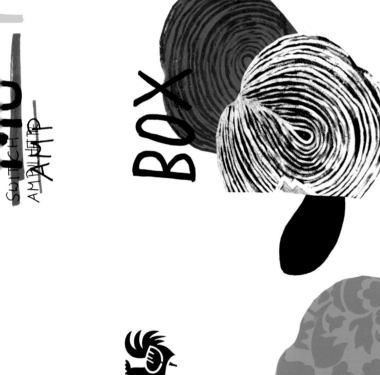

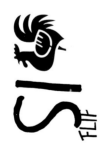

SI
FLIP

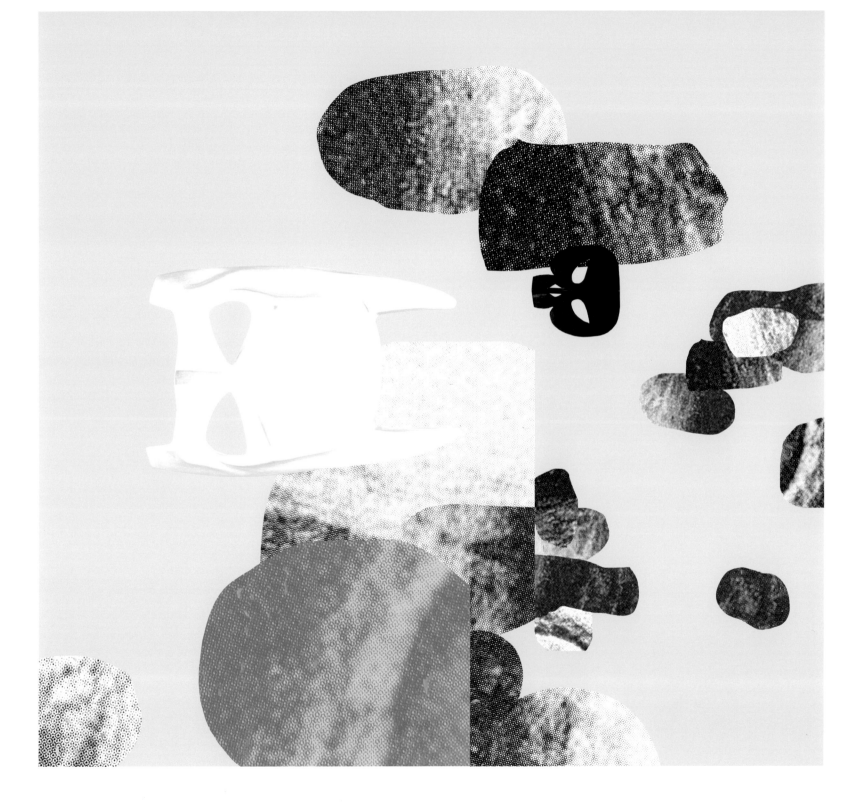

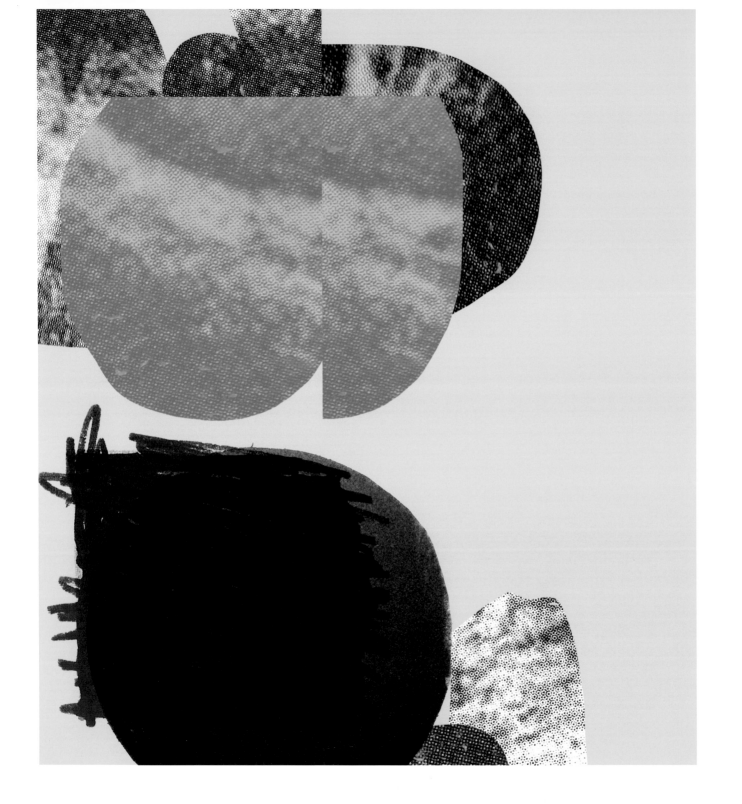

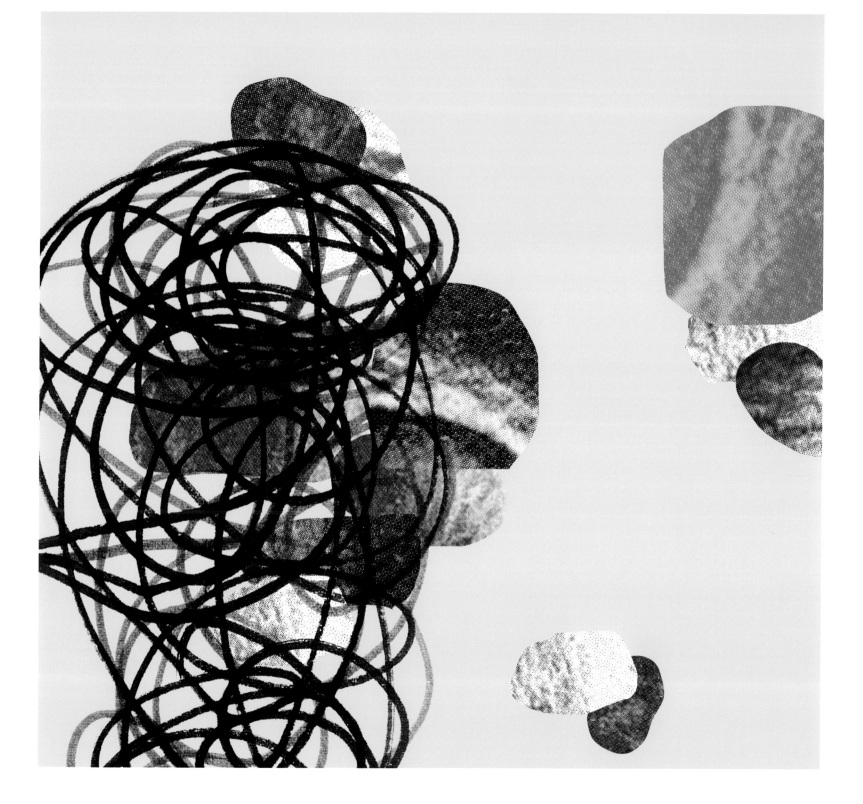

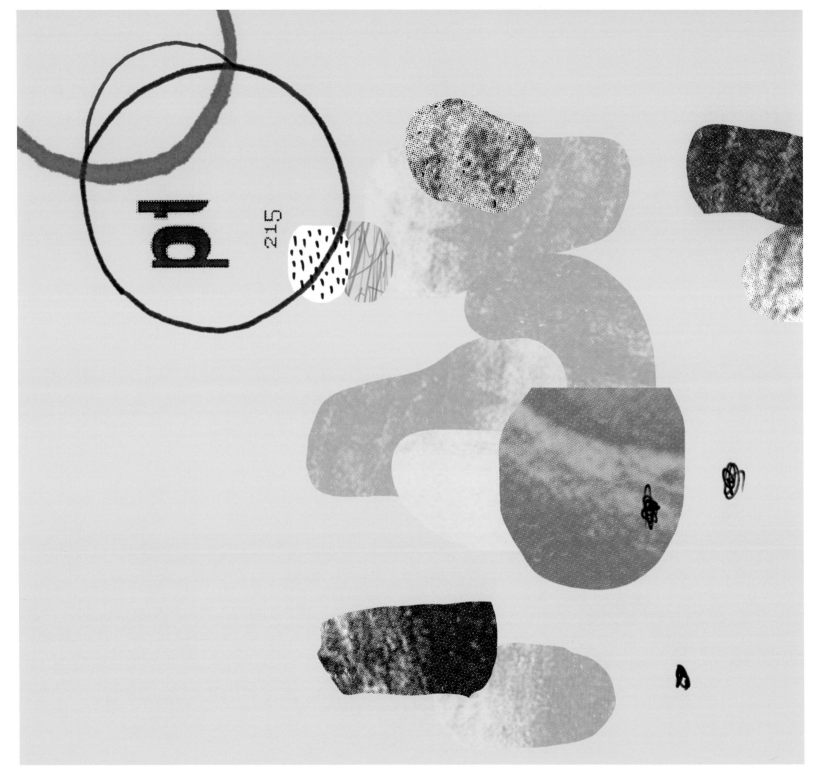

215

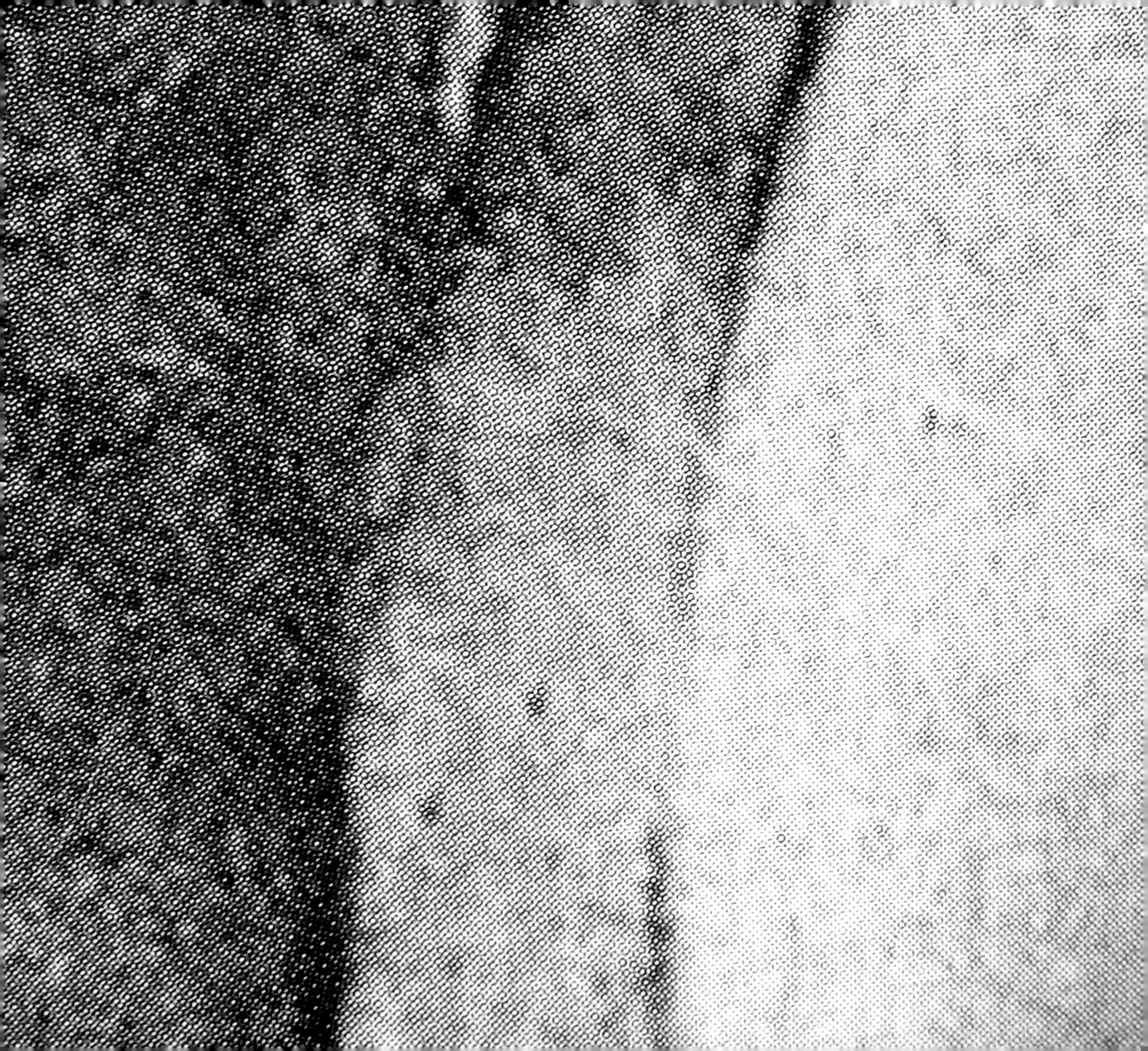

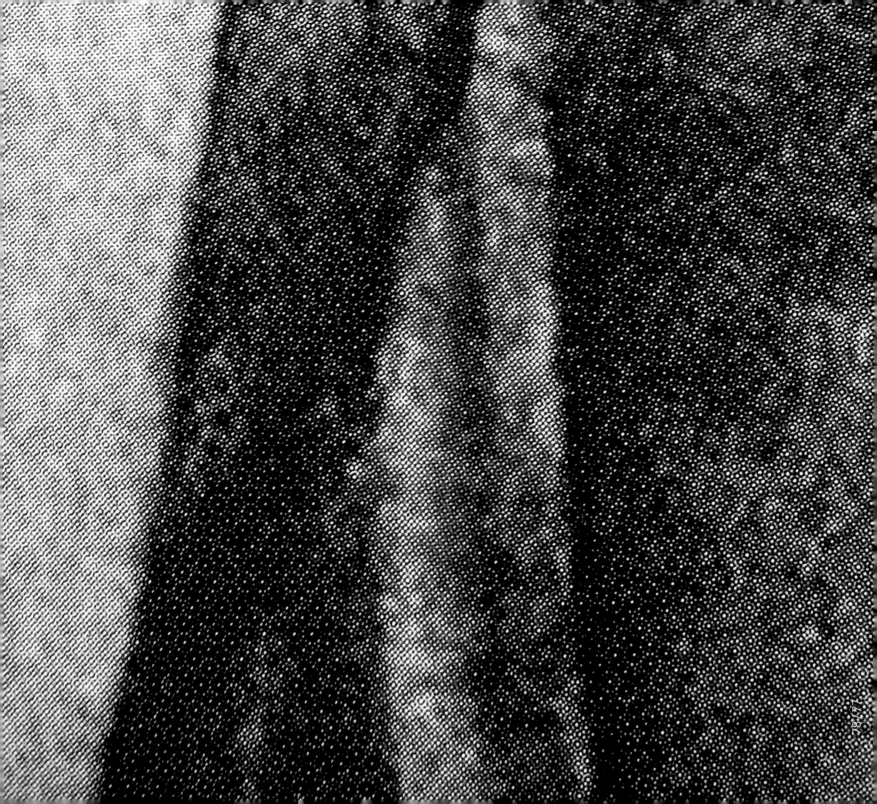

78/77

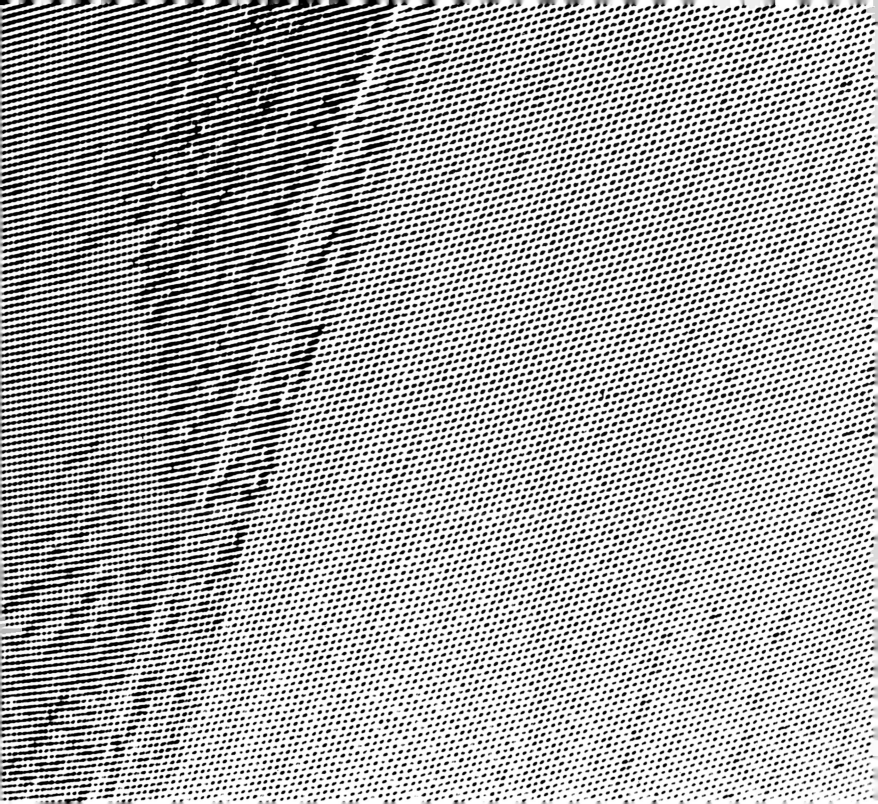

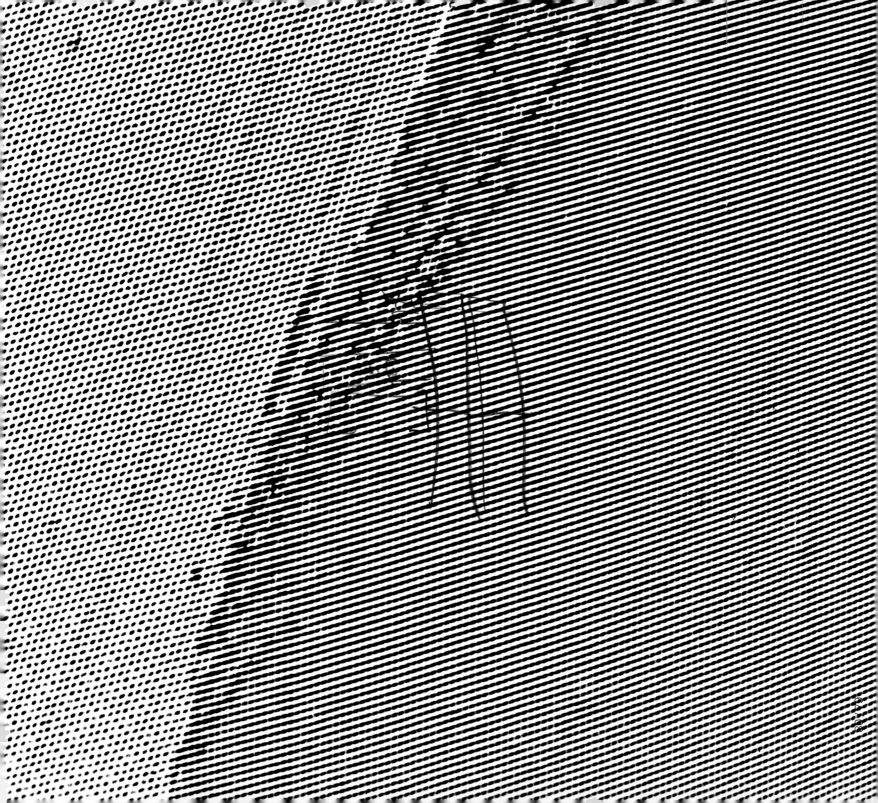

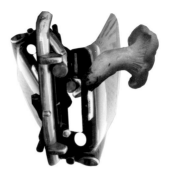
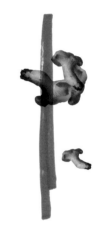

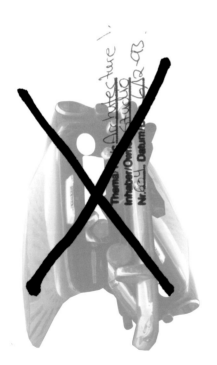

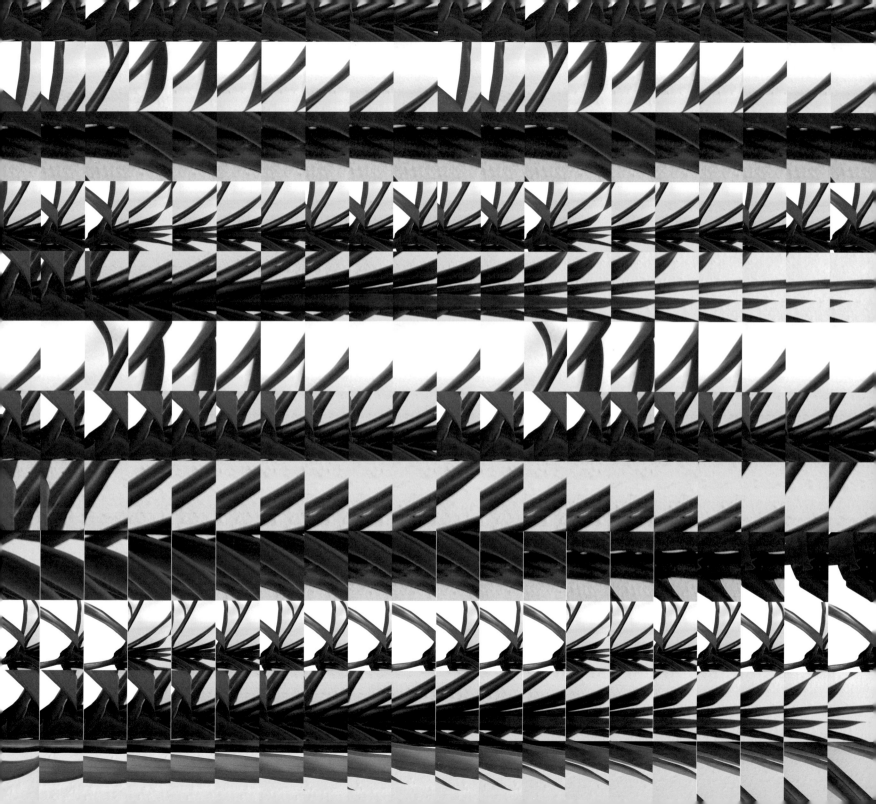

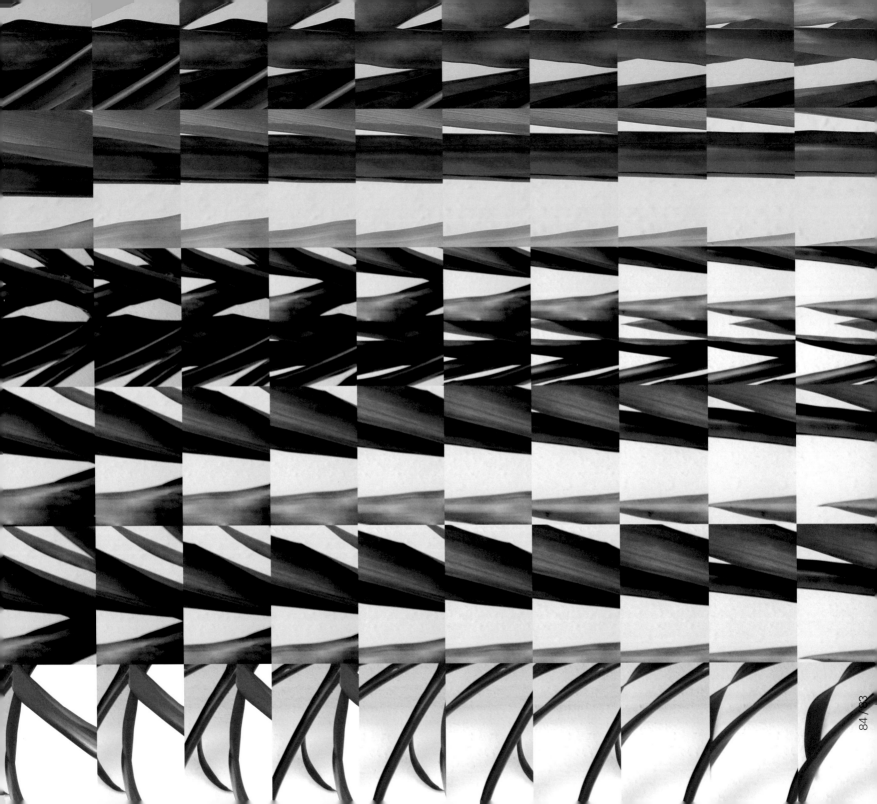

84 / 83

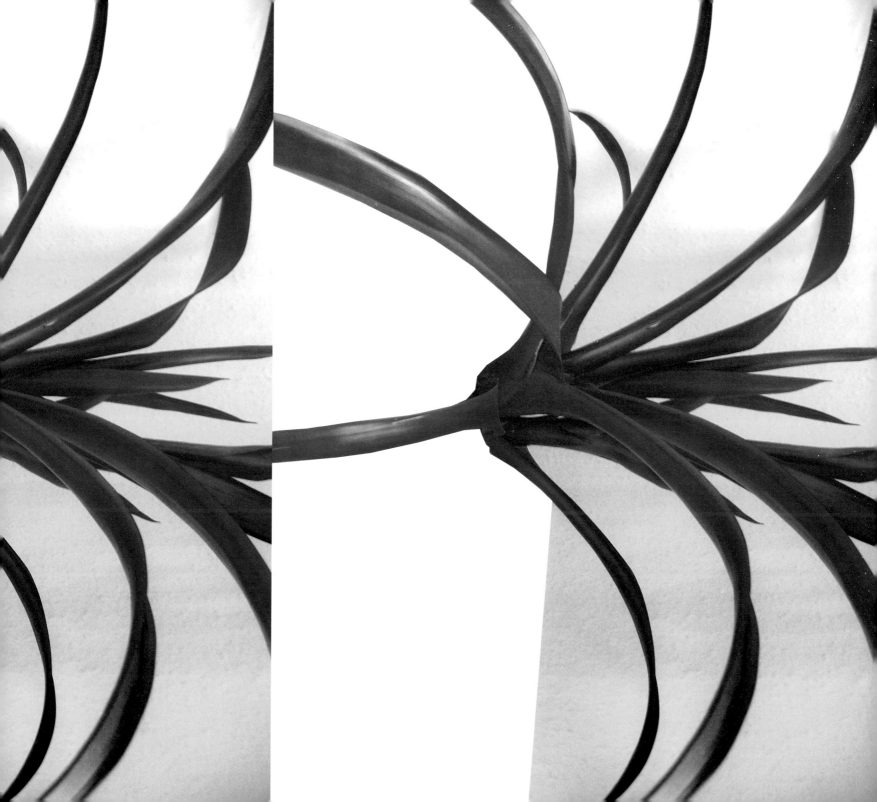

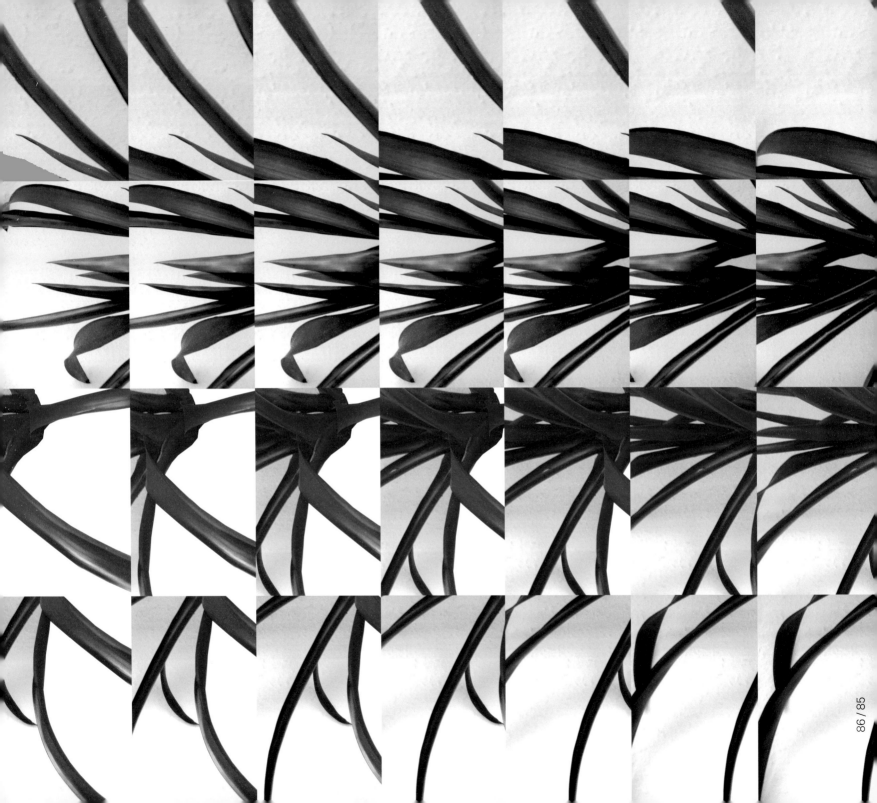

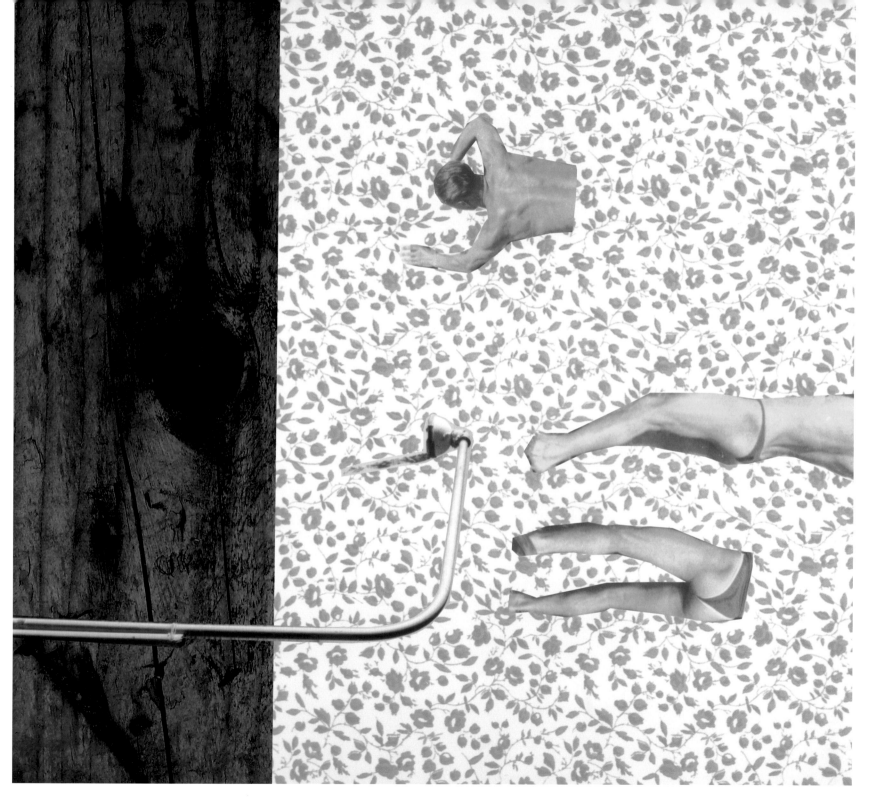

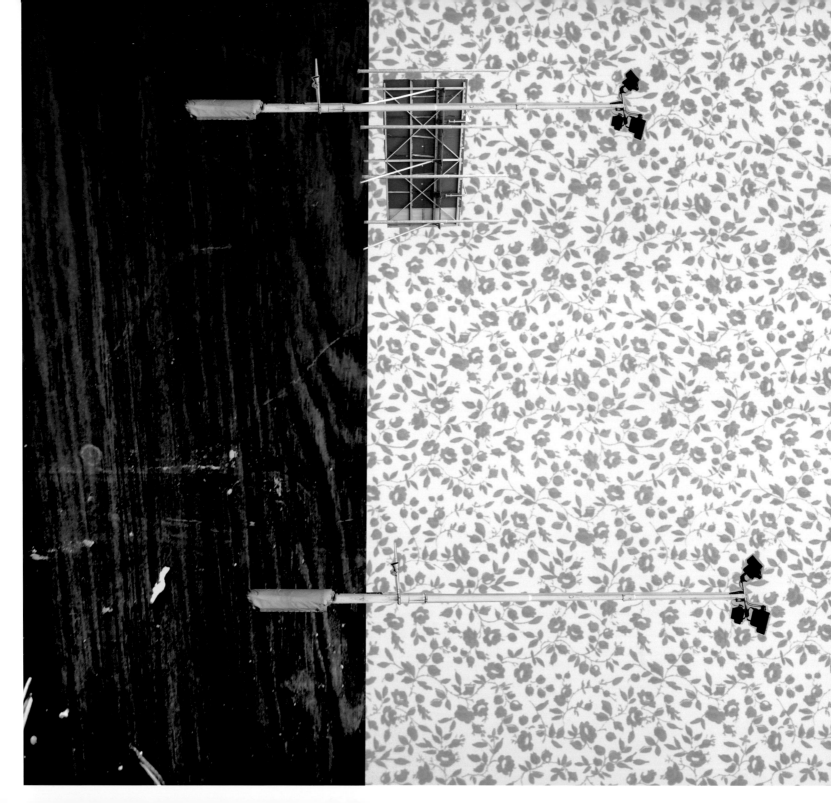

88/87

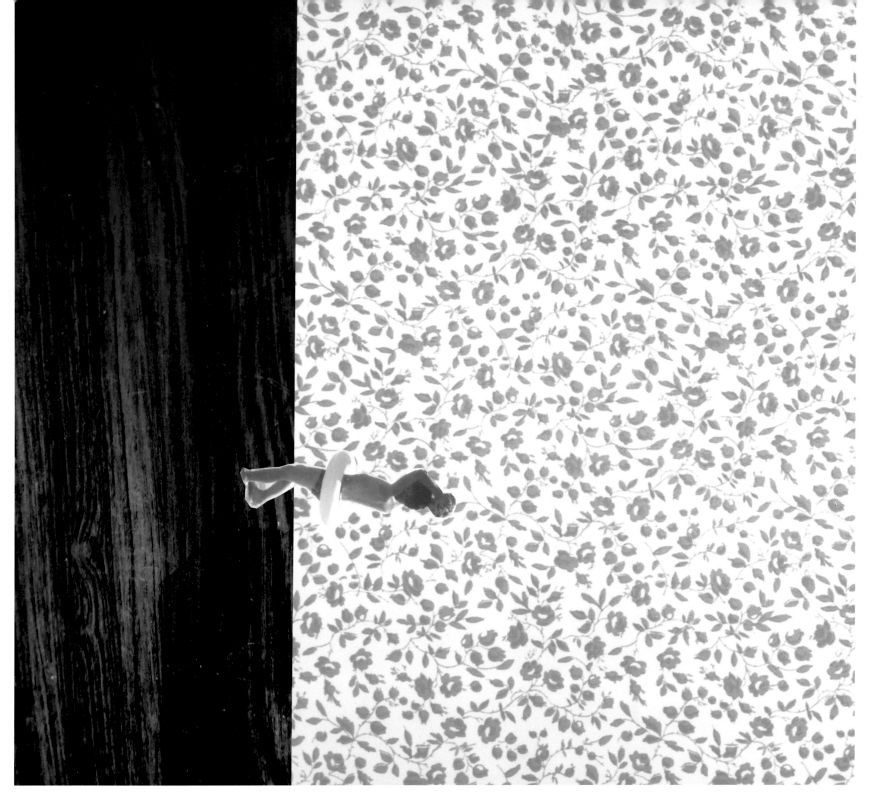

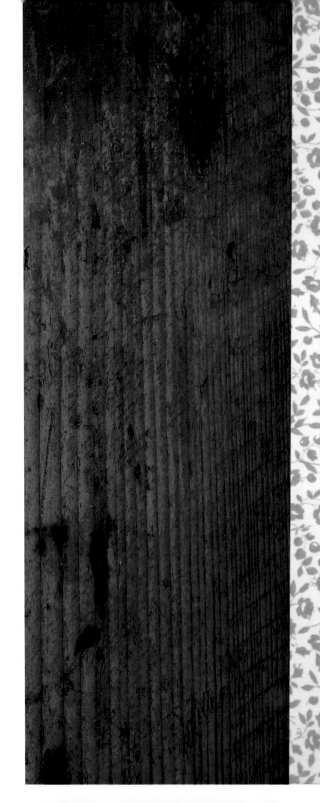
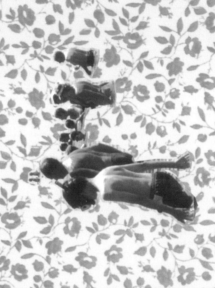
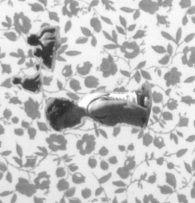

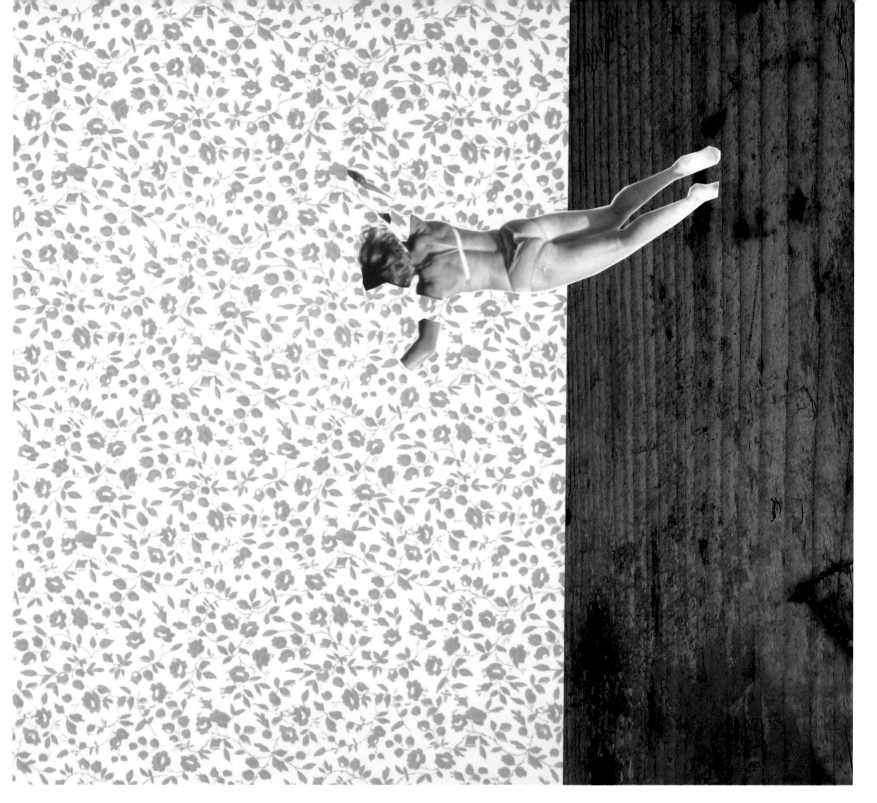

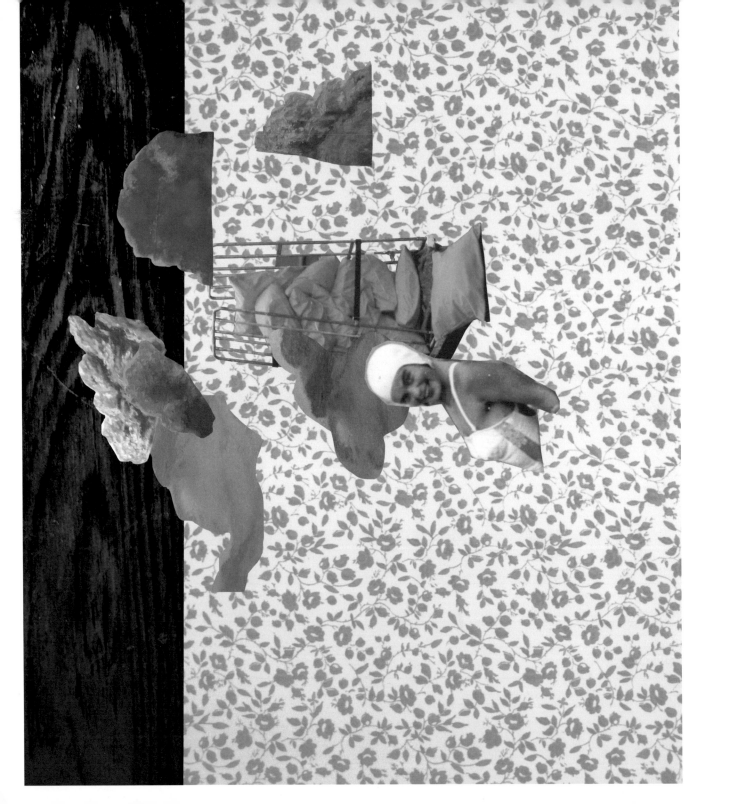

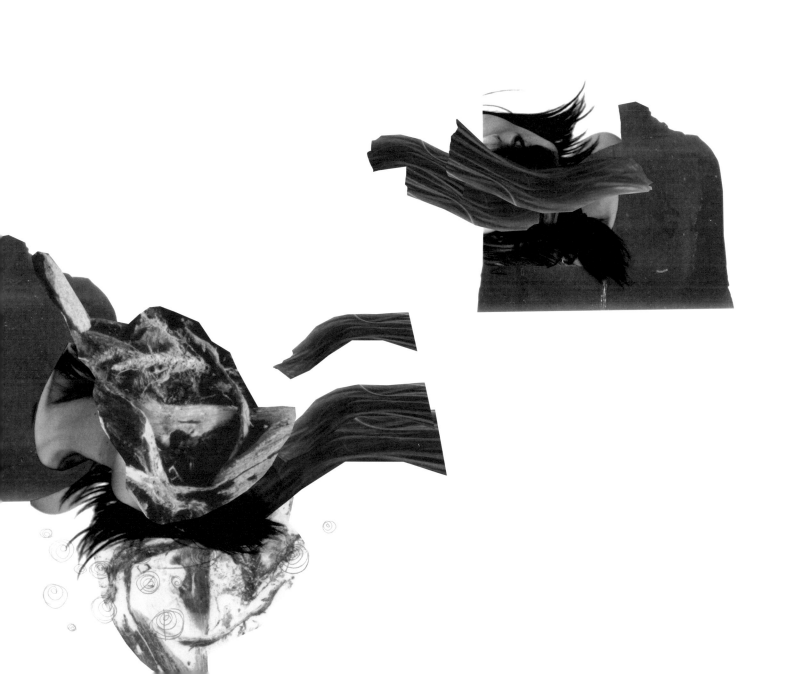

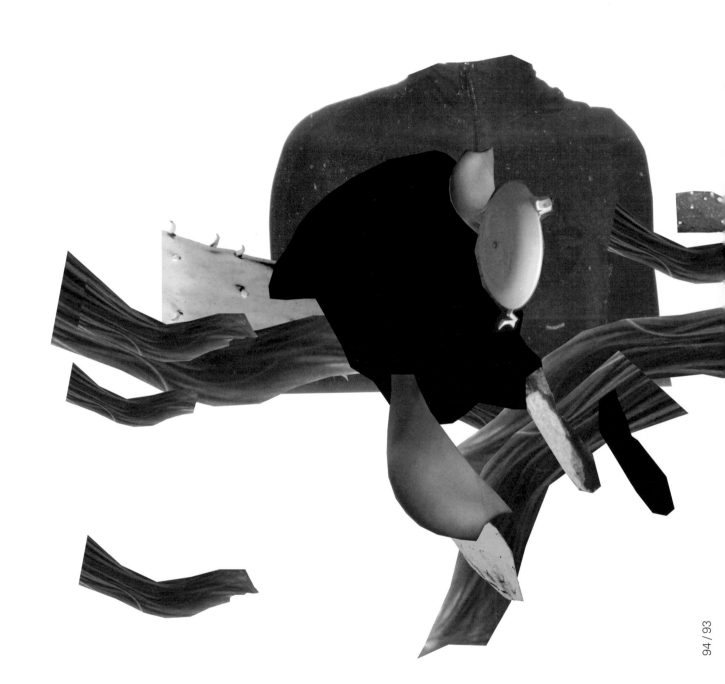

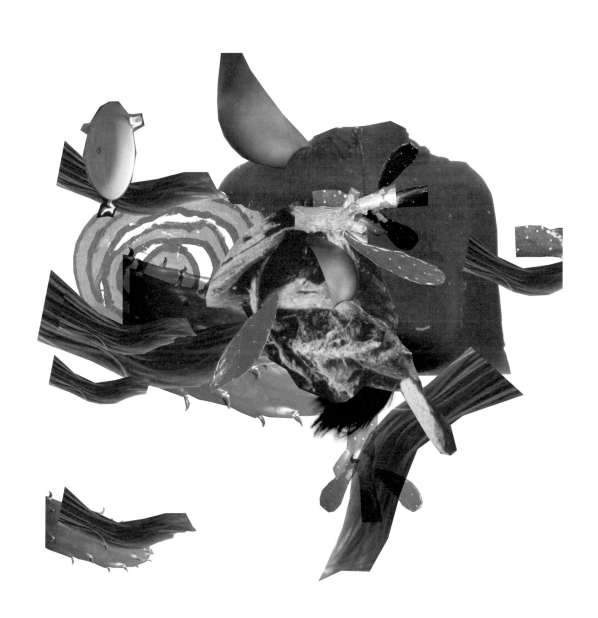

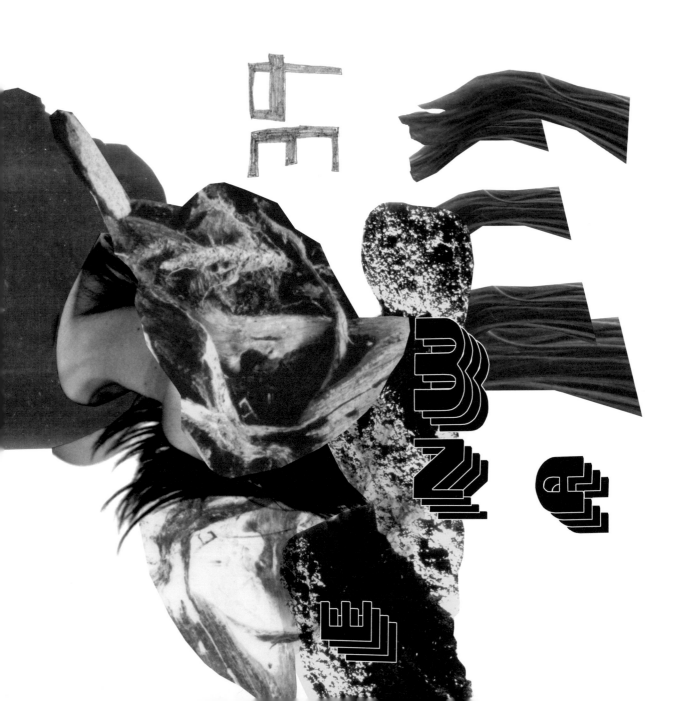

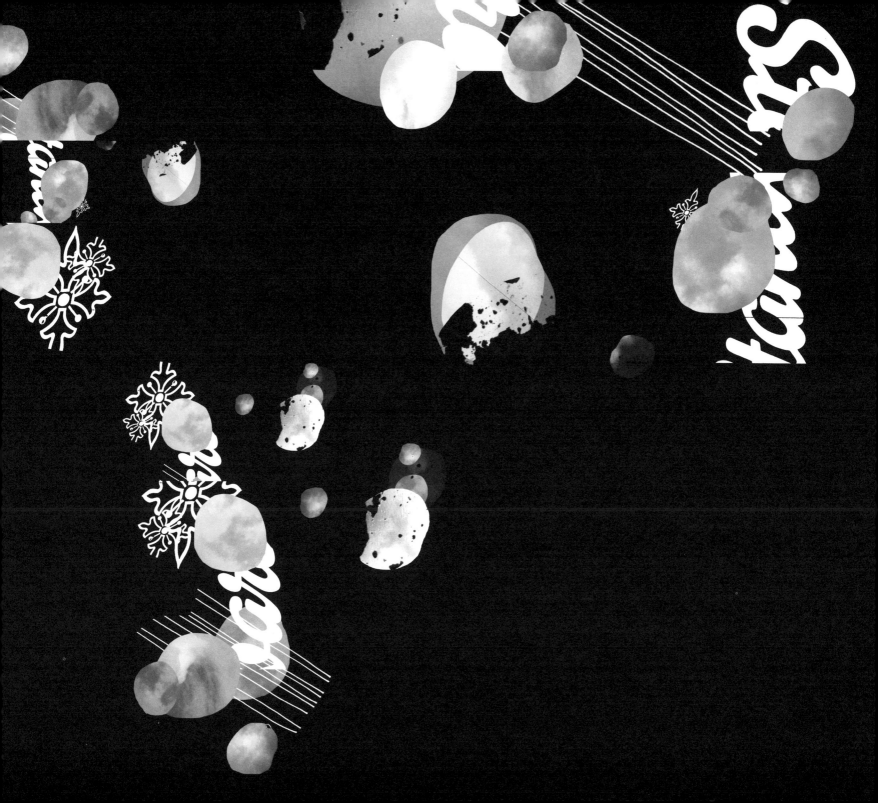

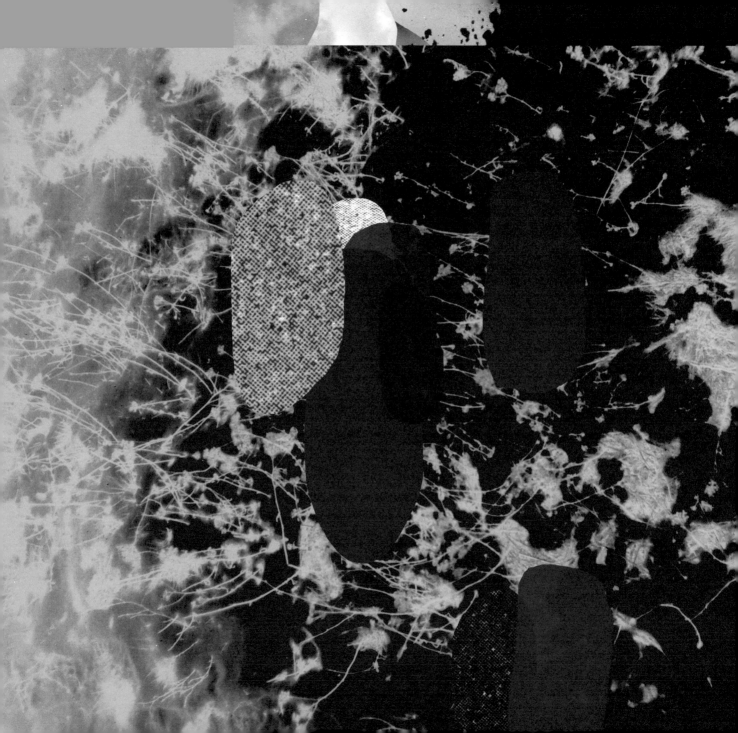

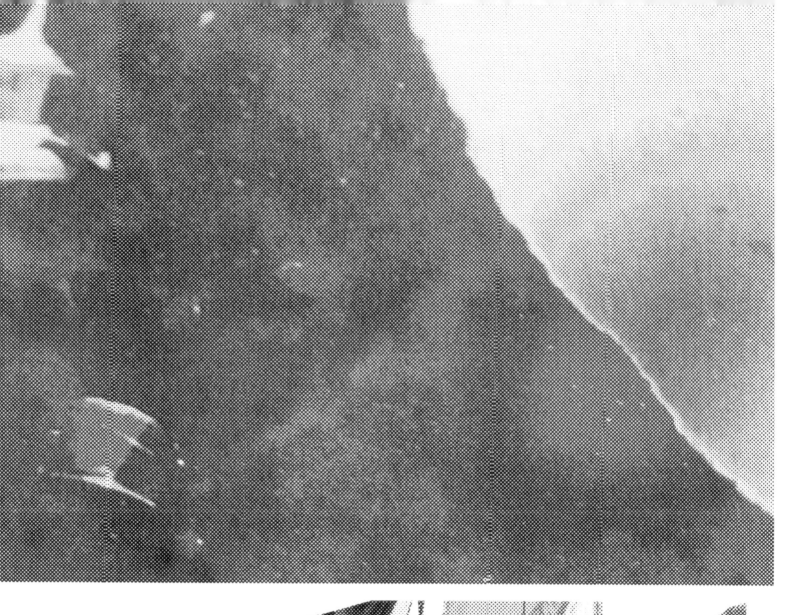
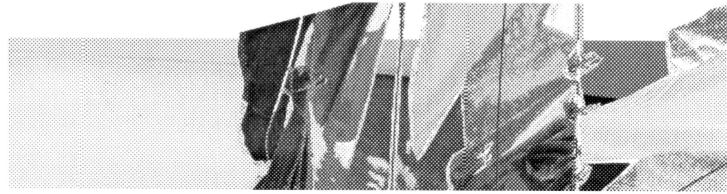

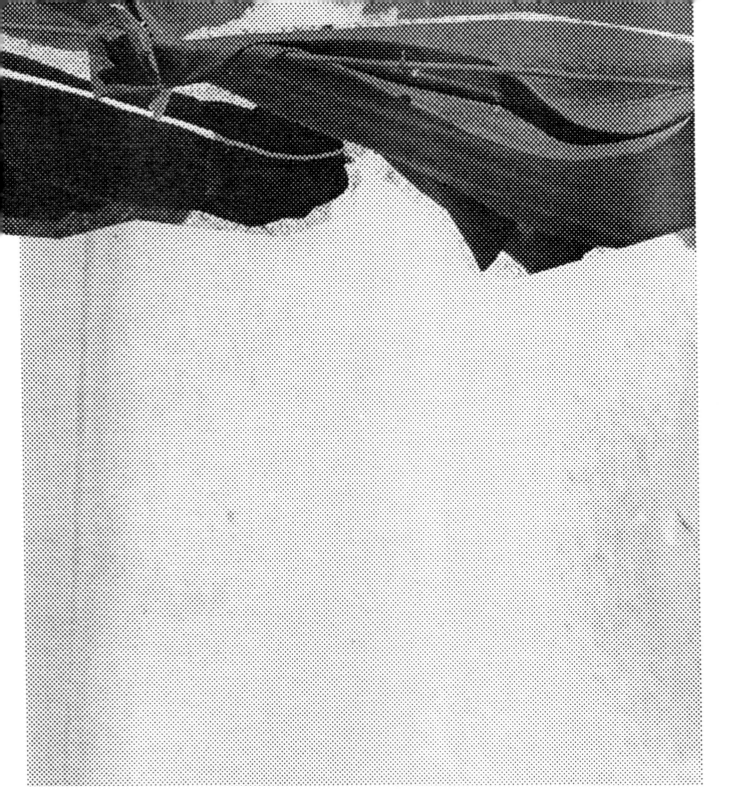

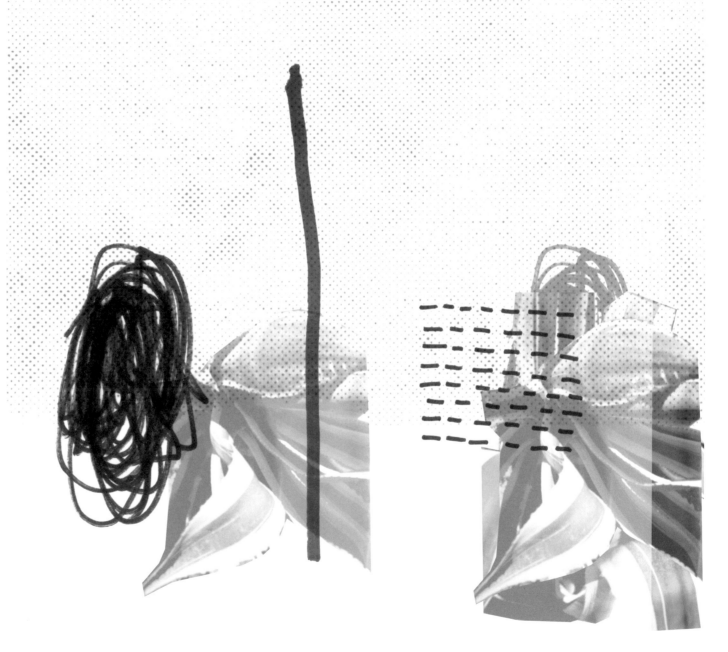

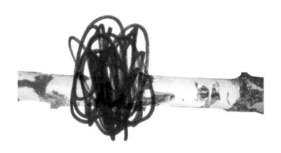

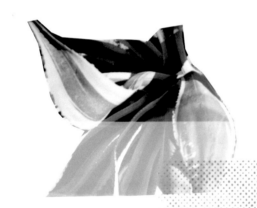

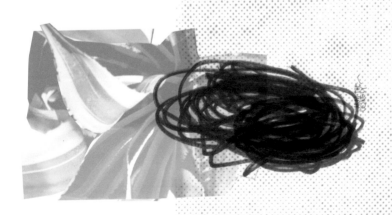

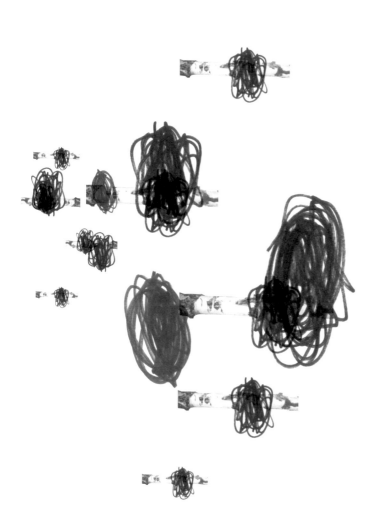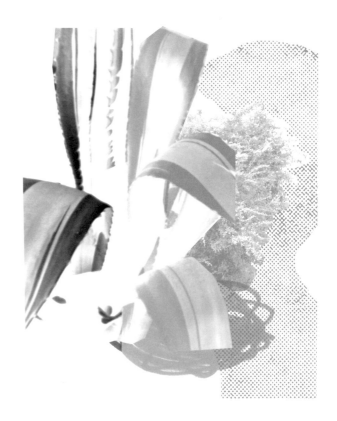

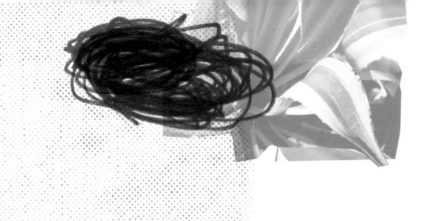

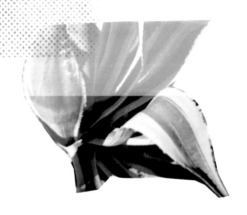

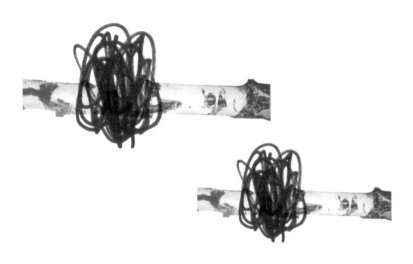

58)
Theodor W. Adorno: *Introduction to Sociology (Problems of Moral Philosophy)* [Einleitung in die Soziologie] (trans. E. Nosowa)

54)
Umberto Eco

55)
Roger Behrens

56)
Wolfgang Tillmans

All reification is forgetting, and criticism is more or less equivalent to remembering; i.e., activating within the phenomena that which made them what they are and thus the awareness of the possibility that they could also have become another and therefore can be another. 58)

The practice of observation leads to theoretical approaches in that it sharpens the senses and power of judgement, increasing one's capacity to combine different viewpoints and to think multi-dimensionally. Reaching a reforming of knowledge as a consequence of the isolation and dissolution of forms for the purposes of analysis – as well as a persistent, successive reconstruction, reintegration, and synthesis – a missing or unreachable consensus between interlaced levels involves the possibility of thinking about facts and conditions in an alternative way: failure, conflict, and wrong turns taken can be more useful and beneficial than clear and positive results. The principle consists of starting somewhere and not remaining idle from worry, but establishing a pattern of working through and trying to comprehend what in the end can only be partly perceived. Concentrating on production as a method in and of itself demonstrates the impossibility of being able to adequately deal with the defined requirements, as well as of the claim of being able to understand the world, not successively but simultaneously, with the aid of images. At the most an imprecise approximation is thinkable. It is impossible to apprehend every aspect of the world when the only constant is the instability of the material available for perception.

Only one-tenth of one per cent of what we perceive reaches our consciousness. Even if we could completely understand the individual parts of that material in their entire complexity or could achieve an exchange or transmission of information without loss, it would, so to speak, "overheat" and transcend our perceptional system. The edited content of this book presents an intuitive examination, an attempt to reach convergence and synchronisation, without completely pinpointing either method, material, or receptor.

Modern science does not hold that what is new is always right. On the contrary, it is based on the principle of "fallibilism" … according to which science progresses by continually correcting itself, falsifying its hypotheses by trial and error, admitting its own mistakes – and by considering that an experiment that doesn't work out is not a failure but is worth as much as a successful one because it proves that a certain line of research was mistaken and it is necessary either to change direction or even to start over from scratch. 54)

Differences are calculated stereotypes; even objective differentiation is in and of itself conformity. 55)

A concept of differentiation is not introduced to establish separate and divided independent identities which delimit or defend themselves, each against the other, but in order to fuse them with the outlines of others in an interdependent coexistence that simulates the rudiments of a neural network.

But maybe part of my idea of nothingness is that ultimately everything is pretty much the same in terms of physical presence. In other words, even the most uninteresting stuff … is actually physically as present as a diamond, or as a person. 56)

57)
Niklas Luhmann: *Ecological Communication* [Ökologische Kommunikation] (trans. John Bednarz)

53)
Carl Einstein

The code of scientific truth and falsity is directed specifically toward a communicative processing of experience, i.e., of selections that are not attributed to the communicators themselves. The intervention of personal qualities and circumstances are treated as disturbing noises and, like other 'accidents', eliminated if they do not lead to valuable discoveries of truths or falsities. ...

The scientific code of truth and falsity is directed specifically towards the *acquisition* of new scientific knowledge. The mere recording, preserving and retrieving of knowledge has required little human effort ever since the invention of printing. ...

Similarly, scientific analysis does not serve to solve problems but to multiply them. It begins from problems that are solved or from problems having a chance of solution and inquires further. ...

The way that science goes about its task rests on a *differentiation of theory and method*. Theories (research programs resulting from research programs) externalize the internal results of scientific work, i.e., apply them to the world that can be experienced by everyone. On the other hand, methods apply the code, i.e., make sure that the results can be distributed according to the values 'true' and 'false'. In this case the test procedures of decision theory, game theory and statistics provide only provisional certainties. ...

Theories represent the openness, while methods—through the exclusion of third values—the closure of systems. 57)

Pictures only mean something to us when they destroy reality and recreate it. That means that pictures are instruments with which to strengthen a crisis. They should not portray anything, but just be. ... Pictures are living things, temporary fragments. We thumb our noses at immortality: one should not suppress death – this living force – with expressions of aestheticism. 53)

When saving memories from sinking into oblivion and uncovering, recalling, and conserving data that have been spilt, lost, restored, and sorted out, the more one knows, the more one is able to see. The images manifest themselves against the backdrop of what has been lost without being too obvious or persistent. Questions arise about how the mind retains information, which criteria describe a selection, what happens when things disappear, blur, bleach out, or lose their poignancy. For a reliable estimation of a situation of the most objective kind, it is necessary not to rely overly much on one's personal moral and ethical attitudes. Making comparisons forces an integration of the newly perceived into the old systems. Explicitly showing off one's personal motives and reasons or flaunting one's genuine feelings is counterproductive. Unusual occurrences are valuable only when they are not out of all proportion and similarities to the already processed material can be found. Personal knowledge, experiences, social status, life concepts, and cultural and economic background influence the individual's view of the world in a conse-

<u>Messages are complex forms arising from a sequence of elements chosen from a repertoire. Messages are measured by a quantity of information which is the originality, that is, the quantity of unpredictability (unforeseeability) that they represent.</u> 50)

<u>Aesthetic form is the objective organization of all appearance within the artwork to form eloquent consistency. It is the violent synthesis of the distracted, which it nevertheless preserves as that which it is …, and therefore in fact the expression of truth.</u> 52)

Visual details present themselves respectively as single parts organised into a spatial, two-dimensional system without the restriction of a continual succession. Analogue to arising memories, they can appear and influence the present at any given moment, whether desired or not. This kind of visual communication is an intermediate stage, an unobstructed space of potentiality including a variable number of possible states and combinations thereof.

Each little detail is but a small part and a single aspect of an immense spectrum of several simultaneous processes. How can the right image for something be found when it is composed of and formed by a combination of volatile influences?

Something new happens long before our perception has adjusted to the consequences of what has just occurred: the more things happen, the faster the adjustments to be made. Decisions and rules set up within a work situation are established to be abolished immediately. Looking at something is a respectful way of appropriating it, because the distance between subject and object can not be dissolved; and the viewer only takes a copy away from the original by means of neuronal stimuli, without affecting the object of regard itself. The moment of observation reveals itself as a paradoxical act combining activity and self-awareness, at the same time resulting in an alienation from oneself as a social being when recognising the opposite other.

The proposed method is not reducible to measurability, exact countability, or rigid categories. It works as a descriptive approximation of knowledge that has to be continuously reviewed and rearranged, as opposed to authoritarian solutions or the simple "yes/no" or "good/bad" statements characteristic of binary decisions. Making provisions for the varying weights of things and opinions, assessing the forces, balancing the power, and pursuing the complicated paths of attention while concentrating on nuances – and thus avoiding a rigid and statutory hierarchical system of categorisation – the dimensioning and amplitude of the layers of relationships and discourses can not be described in their totality. Variety is even "fore-feelable". As a personal, intuitive selection of visual impulses, no visual material is able to reach the complexity of reality, no matter which rules it is following. What then can such an intuitive cataloguing accomplish? As one divides visual material into its component parts and rearranges objects and facts, proceeding like a scientist in simulating a delimited partition of the world, the method of analysis has to be general and transparent in order to unfold an understandable system for the recipient and as a consequence results in taking a position.

Every choice generalises, decontextualises, confirms, and establishes artificial frames of reference. The system of subdivision itself is not absolute, and not even very important. According to Ernst H. Gombrich in *Art and Illusion*, it would be impossible to establish order among our impressions without categories. Strangely enough, what these categories look like plays no important role. They do not necessarily have to be "user-friendly". Their structures can easily be adapted to our needs. If the structures are flexible and elastic, an initial vagueness can even be advantageous.

51)
Maurice Merleau-Ponty: Phenome-
nology of Perception (trans. Paul
Kegan)

Existence has no fortuitous attributes, no
content which does not contribute towards
giving it its form; it does not give admittance
to any pure fact because it is the process by
which facts are drawn up. 51)

Dependent upon conditions, cohesiveness and adhesiveness between borders, contact and friction, and rejections and transitions, carving out individual forms does not indicate a dissociation, but a relationship within a group of other elements that is described within a whole system of equivalents. Single forms are consequently non-decorative and contain a possibility of meaning. Loose associative relationships are favoured over a random collection, suggesting a meaning that is the implicit interpretation of the image-maker, but which will be additionally enriched and fortified by the observer during the viewing process. In handling the basic material provided by nature and culture, one can extract from the complex and manifold realities of the world one single, more or less phrased and articulated reality. In a relational system of comparison, form emerges from noise because it possesses a different degree of material (internal) coherence.

Noise, on the other hand, is a disorganised flickering and the purest state of the material. A certain immateriality is generated through the interspersion of symbols, abstract elements, omissions, duplications, patterns, and sequences. At the same time, this immateriality is systematically compared with concrete reality. Every manifestation of a form is also an expression of its perishability and transitoriness.

Familiar and easily comprehensible visual findings – concrete and common, props and motifs – transferred on a level of comparison of contents and appearance, are able to bring individual entities into correlation. Flexible systems, not primarily conceived as referential systems, are a constant cause of confrontation and encourage a sense of the uniqueness of each occurrence and a passion for the recognisable, a focussed feeling for reality, and an interest in closely examining things again, even if it seems that there is nothing more to be seen. In an obsessive readiness to become involved and look at the same things repeatedly from different positions, more than fearing the endless amount of new build-ups, one sees the potential for volatility and variability.

According to the theory of the "calculus of indications" by George Spencer Brown in his *Laws of Form*, every observation is based on a distinction and the definition of form is "the unity of distinction". Form is therefore not a beautiful shape, but the difference, comparison, and relationship of a thing to its surroundings.

49)
Terry Eagleton: Literary Theory

... a shift from seeing the poem or novel as a
closed entity, equipped with definite meanings which it is the critic's task to decipher,
to seeing it as irreducibly plural, an endless
play of signifiers which can never be finally
nailed down to a single center, essence or
meaning. 49)

asking for answers in the form of further experiences that confirm or disprove the initial assumptions. Consciousness has an intentional focus and is purposeful, sense-oriented, and driven by discretion and particular motives. Every development of concrete visuals implies the loss of an immense amount of material because of its being limited to a selection. Every specification implies the existence of an infinite amount of excluded material. The more exact, elaborate, and concrete a method of analysis is, and the higher its ability to provide reliable, calculable results, the more the amount and variety of possible perception is reduced. There is always more left to say than has already been said.

An intuitive but transparent analysis of the processes of internalising the world and re-externalising the processed material may also help to demystify the contemplative and representative concepts, as well as the value of that material, hence removing the lofty, slick mythology surrounding the production of art and design.Vagueness and indefiniteness ideally conserve the volatileand fragile poetic allure hardly to be found in something executed to perfection, and therefore reveal the humility and human imperfection in the aesthetics of attempt and failure.

48)
Niklas Luhmann: *Ecological Communication* [Ökologische Kommunikation] [trans. John Bednarz]

System differentiation makes possible the establishment and reduction of complexity. The system can place possibilities within the environment and view what is found there as a selection from numerous possibilities. It can project something negative and use this to identify something positive. It can form expectations and be surprised. ...
        The difference technique can be used by these systems because distinctions, negations, possibility projects and information are and remain purely internal and because, in this respect, no environmental contact is possible. In this way the systems remain dependent on autopoiesis, on a continual self-renewal of their elements by their elements, but because information and information expectations, i.e., structures are obtained by means of difference projections, this closure is openness at the same time. For the system can experience itself as its difference from the environment by means of the very same difference technique. 48)

45)
Larry Clark: *Ken Park*

Trivial occurrences prove and confirm to us both our own existence and that of reality. Constant and recurrent visual impulses grant security and tranquillity because the experiences can be sorted into a relational system. Their arrangement (in this book as well as in one's own mind) contains one accentuated possibility out of innumerable others. An examination of the optical field must converge as much as possible at the processes of perception: simultaneously contemporary and historical, close and distant, excluding and containing, exposed and hidden. Its transitoriness demands a permanent occupation with it and a constant verification process and can evoke a sense of melancholic yearning.

I can't dream of other places. I can't picture in my head what they look like. Everything I think about looks like here. 45)

The attempt to make life distinct through incidental means of perception leads to an undefined clarity: the haziness at the edges of one's visual field contains possibilities for points of contact with open systems. The intersections between the observer and the creator of the images force a transfer of information and a potential discourse. Nothing is fixed, no knowledge is "objective", everything is context. Everyone is at once spectator and actor. Knowledge exists in an established form that articulates the material within a social context and allows it to be reviewed and revised at any given moment.

43)
Merlin Carpenter

For me, if a piece of information can be traded, then it's not worth trading. 43)

Transcribing the seen, learned, and experienced into communication means making a selection in a complex act of exclusion. Every selection decontextualises and constructs, generalises, confirms, and carves out (id)entities that necessarily differ from the reality of the basic material, no matter which criteria are followed. A formal construct is introduced that is reusable and applicable for an exchange of content, similar to the way language defines comprehensible units of meaning. It is unavoidable that the formal structure remain imprecise, vague, and out of focus compared to reality. A selection consists of an act of marking and highlighting, which serves to emphasise and which for inscrutable reasons is problematical and therefore calls attention to itself.

Exclusions are implicit and able to come to the surface at any time: some information is probably not of interest except at the specific moment of selection, which is no more than a temporary tagging or marking of a specific component in a space that has not yet been worked on.

And what would thinking be if it did not constantly confront chaos? 46)

Meaning is a representation of world complexity that is actualizable at any moment. The discrepancy between the complexity of the actual world and consciousness's capacity for apprehension or communication can be bridged only when the scope of the actual intention is restricted and all else is rendered potential, i.e., reduced to the status of mere possibility.

There is no such thing as a 'stimulus inundation' since the neurophysiological apparatus already screens off conciousness drastically, and the operative medium of meaning has to work very hard to permit something that is well digested to become actual. ...

The system introduces its *own distinctions* and, with their help, grasps the states and events that appear to it as *information*. Information is thus a purely system-internal quality. ... 47)

46)
Gilles Deleuze, Félix Guattari: *What Is Philosophy?* (trans. Janis Tomlinson)

47)
Niklas Luhmann: *Ecological Communication* [Ökologische Kommunikation] (trans. John Bednarz)

44)
Richard Buckminster Fulle

Look closely and comprehensively at these pictures. Integrate your reactions with all your spontaneous recalls of the other experiential information of your life as well as of other lives as reported to you. Think and think some more. 44)

dreas Gursky

Richard Sennett: *The Fall of Public Man*

Jeff Wall

Günther Anders: *Ketzereien* [Heresies]

41)

delimited by spatial borders, facilitate acting clearly within its insularity. This limitedness brings about actions having a certain freedom and immunity within these borders and presents the possibility of allowing complexity without a complete loss of overview. The primary initial intention of converging the images with the outside world, while maintaining a disregard for achieving any particular aim or reaching any specific target within the established rules, warrants an open output, a certain distancing from oneself and one's needs, longings, and satisfactions, and locates a fertile ground for increasing one's willingness to take risks and not withdraw into an illusion of security. These all constitute the basic requirements for taking action. Rather than believing in monolithic verities and pretending for a period of time that all differences in moral codes, judgement, class distinction, origin, and education have already been abolished, certain untenable rules of fabricated social realities are necessary and useful to achieve a particular communicational level among people.

To understand the spectator as a public figure we have finally to understand him outside the theater, on the streets. For here his silence is serving a larger purpose; here he is learning that his codes for interpreting emotional expression are also codes for isolation from others; here he is learning a fundamental truth of modern culture, that the pursuit of personal awareness and feeling is a defense against the experience of social relations. ...

Today, impersonal experience seems meaningless and social complexity an unmanageable threat. By contrast, experience which seems to tell about the self, to help define it, develop it, or change it, has become an overwhelming concern. In an intimate society, all social phenomena, no matter how impersonal in structure, are converted into matters of personality in order to have a meaning. Political conflicts are interpreted in terms of the play of political personalities; ...

Faced with complexity, people reach for some inner, essential principle amid the complex, because converting social facts into symbols of personality can only succeed once the complex nuances of contingency and necessity are removed from a scene. ...

Interchanges in society were disclosures of personality. It did so by framing the perception of personality in such a way that the contents of personality never crystallized, thus engaging men in an obsessive and end less search for clues as to what others, and themselves, were "really" like. Over the course of the hundred years, social bonds and social engagement have receded in the face of inquiry about "what am I feeling?" 42)

The less you know, the more you look. 38)

No art-philosophical notion is more wrong than the idea that the respective artwork is an "expression" of the particular "mood" of the composer. ... Mood is not the origin of the work, but its effect. 39)

Different and diffuse particles of the world propel themselves into the visual field and behave during the perceptive process as if they were on an alternative level of reality. The differing appearances of the objects deserve a distinct investment of effort, concentration, and attention by means of the perceptive processes.

Standardisation and categorisation are central prerequisites for a perceptual experience. A certain amount of anonymity and abstraction should be introduced; and in the same way, unusual emotional experiences need to be worked through and shaped so that their integration into a system as a principal condition for perception and interaction can be possible.

37)
Roger Silverstone: *Why Study the Media?*

40)
Georg Wilhelm Friedrich Hegel: *Phenomenology of Spirit* [Phänomenologie des Geistes] [trans. E. Nosowa]

A contingency of all phenomena to which no exception can be taken: all that appears does so in the light of the possibilities of its equivalent – as neither necessary nor impossible. That which is known is not recognised because it is known. 40)

Visual details are presented respectively as single parts and organised in a spatial two-dimensional system without the restriction of a constant and linear succession: like memories or dreams they can arise and influence the present at any moment, whether desired or at times unwished for and beyond one's control. This kind of visual communication is an intermediate stage, an unobstructed place of potentiality and variety offering an infinite number of possible states and combinations. Every little detail is a manifestation of one small, single aspect of an indescribable number of processes and problems, all happening simultaneously. It is complicated to find a single image for something that reveals itself as a composite and volatile combination of the influences of the basic material offered by the world. Something new happens long before our perception has adjusted to the consequences of what has just finished happening. The more things happen, the faster they become. Decisions and rules are established only to be abolished immediately afterwards.

So let us grant, then, that experience is indeed shaped. Acts and events, words and images, impressions, joys and hurts, even confusions, become meaningful in so far as they can be related to each other within some, both individual and social, framework: a framework which, albeit tautologically, gives them meaning. Experience is a matter both of identity and difference. It is both unique and shareable. It is both physical and psychological. So much is clear and indeed banal and obvious. But how is experience shaped and how does the media play a role in its shaping?
Experience is framed, ordered and interrupted. It is framed by prior agendas and previous experiences. It is ordered according to norms and classifications that have stood the tests of time and the social. It is interrupted by the unexpected, the unprepared, the event, the catastrophe, by its own vulnerability, by its own inevitable and tragic lack of coherence. Experience is acted out and acted upon. In this sense it is physical, based in the body and on its senses. 37)

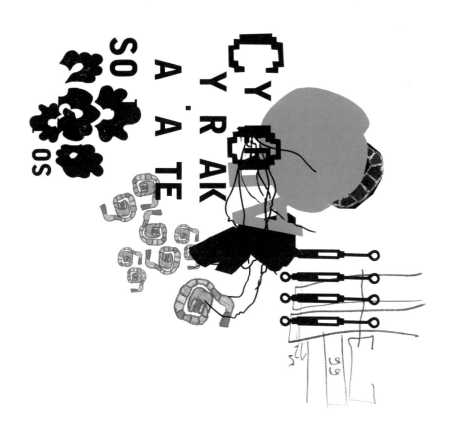

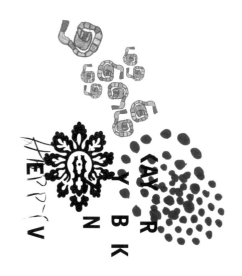

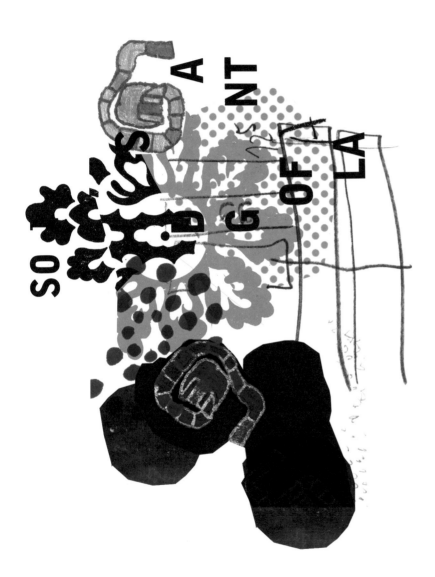

SO THIS A NT
B OF LA
G

movement, every gesture, every second was monopolised by advertising and the media and therefore didn't belong to me. I borrowed those hours from advertising and liked them anyway. 31)

32)
Robert Misik (trans. E. Nosowa)
36)
Chuck Palahniuk: *Lullaby*

Big Brother isn't watching. He's singing and dancing. He's pulling rabbits out of a hat. Big Brother's busy holding your attention every moment you're awake. He's making sure you're always distracted. He's making sure you're fully absorbed 36)

Every gesture that follows a script one is not the author of is commercial property. Whatever we do – even in the most private of private – we are playing cultural scenarios from films that aren't our own. It is one of the great paradoxes of our time: authenticity is considered the highest good, and individuality is the defining ideology – but in the end, everyone wants to be like everyone else. Identity is consumed, and this construction is not only theoretically available to all, but it is for all practical purposes based on (culture industry-produced) role models. 32)

The infiltration of world-wide and nearly real-time imagery into one's daily routines by a continuous sprinkling from the mass media jams one's channels of perception and causes a shift from attentiveness to an accommodative, thoughtless numbness. When confronted with this unmanageable amount of material to evaluate and process, the individual tends to revolve around him or herself, choosing defensive strategies of representation in trying to achieve a voice and to be heard, using standardised forms of self-presentation and established postures. The risk consists of losing the ability to keep an unobstructed view of the external conditions. The number of events that have to be processed becomes unmanageable: added to personal events come a vast number of local and global events, synchronised with a delay of only a few minutes or hours. The individual takes part in human society by retrieving information from the media and is thus affected and becomes overstrained at a distance, without actually getting directly involved. Extreme and shocking reality – catastrophes, terrorist attacks, natural disasters, homicides, and accidents – is presented in the news on a lower and less sophisticated visual level than any sort of action scene in a feature film or any perfectly produced advertising spot: we are drowning in illusions and special effects. Are the perfect formal quality and the equally perfect emotional intimacy and timing of artificial footage that we are fixated on able to impress more than reality itself, and possibly even change our sensory capacities?

33)
Jonathan Friedman: *Cultural Identity and Global Process*; "Globalization and Localization"

The act of identification, the engagement of the person in a higher project, is in one sense an act of pure existential authenticity, but to the degree that it implies a consumption of self-defining symbols that are not self-produced but obtained in the market place, the authenticity is undermined by objectification and potential decontextualisation. Thus while engagement authenticates, its consumption de-authenticates. The only authentic act in side of such a system is an act that encompasses both the authentic and its commodification. 33)

achim Lottman: *Die Jugend von ute [The Youth of Today] (trans. Nosowa)

<u>I always try to get people to focus less, or at least not first, on finding 'meaning', or 'theme' in the work, but to focus on what it is exactly.</u> 34)

28)
A. G. Baumgarten: *Aesthetica*, §483

The value of commodities and goods is no longer defined by the function of the product or the service being provided: lemon-squeezers and advertisements make claim to an artificial cultural value and consequently are nearly intangible and unassailable in the face of criticism.

<u>The probable is that about which we can have no complete certainty, and yet cannot discern anything erroneous. Aesthetic truth is thus in its material meaning: probability.</u> 28)

The moment of working up and displaying the material is a process of rethinking and rearranging the individual parts: thoughts, situations, events, values, promises, memories, influences, hopes, and fears. Reasons are examined and verified, statements rechecked, objections factored in, plans dismissed, and inconsistencies and ambiguities kept if they seem appealing or unclassifiable. The perpetual flow of images is captured artificially for a fraction of a second like a frozen moment of reality and becomes accessible and vulnerable, thus inviting criticism and accepting responsibility for the surrounding world.

the all-marketable world

35)
Albert Camus, *The Myth of Sisyphus*

<u>There is but one truly serious philosophical problem and that is suicide.</u> 35)

29)
Marshall McLuhan

Just as necessary as inspecting the attractive perfection of shiny surfaces and exposing and reflecting upon the strategies of the market is a further examination of the ostentation of a chavvy anti-culturalism as well as an elitist culturalism of the well-heeled, and the consequential intellectual arrogance; the over-reliance on economic and political progress; and the underlying intolerance of an educated bohemia that is averse to dealing with the banal, boring, monotonous, trivial, and worthy or that of specialists who are glib in presenting sophisticated and intangible theories and exclusive opinions. Life is too personal to hand over all decisions to the self-appointed experts, for it would be dangerous and irresponsible.

30)
Sarah Morris: *Art Now*

<u>Everybody experiences far more than he understands. Yet it is experience, rather than understanding, that influences behaviour.</u> 29)

<u>The emptiness and flatness reflects the way things are. It's perverse to create a seductive emptiness. The work distorts reality by simplifying experiences into codes and icons.</u> 30)

In times where cultural work – e.g., art or music – is collected through sponsoring by private enterprises aiming to cultivate their own images, every rebellion is soon perfectly appropriated by the prevailing system. Radicalism ends up far removed from being a political vehicle in its aesthetic attitude and posture. Paradoxically, subcultures and anti-cultures can be integrated in a particularly easy way into the global capitalistic culture of goods because of their ability to differentiate.

The goods reveal themselves to be a receptacle for myths deployed to increase business. The consequence consists in selling ideally empty and, therefore, easily adaptable brand experiences representing comfortable, plush, but in the end numb "auras". At its best, even without the need to produce an interfering product or object, the most desired qualities for a design are absolute flexibility and fluidity. This book aims to establish an unjaded point of view, not indulging in complaint or rejection, but advocating flexibility on the part of the consumer, introducing a rudimental concept of perception and deduced communication – a concept of permanent instability that leads to a sensibility to the conditions.

In form, all that is quasi-linguistic in works of art becomes concentrated... Form endeavours to give voice to the individual through the whole. 26)

Commercial competition has pushed forward the most rapid employment of these possibilities [of the fluidification of matter], leading to the multiplication of images and services offered and to the accelerated introduction of the 'new'. At the same time, the lack of a design culture capable of confronting these new technological possibilities has resulted in the dissemination of worthless products. So the potential of the old technology is distributed in the banal forms of gadgets, disposable products, and ephemeral objects lacking any cultural significance. A feeling of generalized transience, an impoverishment of sensory experience, of superficiality and the loss of relations with objects derives from this; we tend to perceive a disposable world: a world of objects without depth that leaves no trace in our memories, but does leave a growing mountain of refuse. 27)

Design is not a neutral tool. ... Design is about decisions and priorities, not equations and logic. Its appropriation by marketing as a sales prefix (e.g. 'designer' furniture), and its recent transformation in mediaspeak from a process into a commodity, are attempts to depoliticize design – just when its political role has become acutely important. 22)

The transformation of the commodity relation into a thing of 'ghostly objectivity' ... stamps its imprint upon the whole consciousness of man; ... And there is no natural form in which human relations can be cast, no way in which man can bring his physical and psychic 'qualities' into play without their being subjected increasingly to this reifying process. 23)

22)
John Thackara: *Design After Modernism*

23)
Georg Lukács: *History and Class Consciousness: Studies in Marxist Dialects* (trans. Rodney Livingstone)

26)
Theodor W. Adorno: *Aesthetic Theory [Ästhetische Theorie]*

27)
Ezio Manzini

24)
Wolfgang Tillmans in an interview
with Neville Wakefield

The endless industry thirst for labels, trends, and fashions turns every individual style into another benign marketing plot. In a way I try to channel attention to take the multi-layeredness of personality and identity. 24)

20)
adapted from John Dewey

25)
adapted from Walter Lippmann: *Drift and Mastery*

The goal of production is to produce free people – free men. 20)

We must consciously deal with life, design its social organisation, change its tools, formulate its methodology ... 25)

It's a commonplace that design implies a commitment to mass production and consumerism and has to satisfy the needs of the market. It has to be populist, producible, easily comprehensible, and follow the principles of supply and demand. Design issues are established and embedded in contemporary cultural, social, and political discourses: designs are exhibited in museums and instrumented to express a certain lifestyle or status or to become the subject of small talk at society events. Hedonistic and smart design objects are valid supports underpinning social positions, reinforcing identities with identical precast perfect fits; indispensable accessories are presented in glamorous, fashionable, and trendy magazines and become irrelevant tomorrow. Everyone is an expert on beauty and aesthetics – meaning "personal preferences and taste". Exhausted in a differentiation of identical products at a level of visual appearance, design redeems almost nothing in contrast with its promises: Pleasing, non-polarising, delightful surfaces reveal and perfectly express the emptiness of the goods, and those blank spaces are filled with a self-referring, ahistorical, and unassailable mythology that serves as an area of projection for representative trends which can easily be exchanged cyclically every season.

A pluralistic and more flexible view of the concepts about life and work replaces the former notion of linear lifelong careers. Social capabilities are overruled by a process of individualisation, leading to a certain amount of autistic behaviour on the part of the individual identities among a multitude of egos. Supposed gained freedom results in a certain emotional immunity and suspiciousness, leading one to construct defensive strategies against external influences and thus to an escape from the cocoon of the social community and its loyalties. Because of the possibility for a person to communicate and interact with the whole world, social responsibilities become lost in the not-abolished emotional distance. One's radius of action is mostly limited to oneself, representing an anonymous, intangible spot within a wide network of relationships. Social contacts are mainly used to monitor feedback on the impact of a personal advertising campaign in furtherance of a self-optimised, constructed, and one-dimensional ego. And for the losers in this game of self-realisation, an esoteric search for sense is an option leading to the same results: well-fed individuals who have difficulty in fitting the marketing suggestions for becoming hyper-real – perfectly shaped, sexually satisfied, emotionally stable, forever young, beautiful, healthy, and with smiling, happy faces

21)
Theodor W. Adorno: *Introduction t*
Sociology [Problems of Moral Philo
sophy] [trans. Edmund Jephcott]

... because in the society in which we live differentiations that appear again and again as if they were of a purely formal nature have the tendency to transform themselves into substance. 21)

HAPPY HOUR
Every Saturday
FROM 7 00 p.m Until 9
Drink two, pay for o

Cancelled, Expected

Arrived, Lost

[coincidence of perception]

identity/difference

linearity and chronological sequence

—

—

—

—

technolo

relation [di inction/contrast]

[one word af r another]

handwritten tters, lists

songs on cas tte mixtapes

mobile homes no parking signs

private prop

teenage angst

watchlist, whishlist

German quality workmanship

more to be confirmed

alibi days

—

—

—

—

perception system

representational system

coin operated

is God lonely?

fragmented and

non-linear

potential of sensual excitement

microaestetics

—

—

sad, old, bad

unlikeable, ugly

unintelligent

unenergetic

bST
MÜ!

critical mass
supermarket. knives
shimmering transitions

contradictions
theoretical basis/workshop

pre-adjustments
picture frame
[idea/reality] prototype

short circuiting cognition
short memory
standard landscapes
enzyme/molecular particles
intermediate deposit
visual catering
dialogue boxes
folding packaging
send it to a friend
retrofuturism

output device

subvers   talk
telepho   conversations
image c   rol

depht s   cture
surface   ructure
interpr   tion
moving   wpoints
issue l   tion
sorrows
comfort
control signs
Gummo Marx
proportion. perspective
sequence and rhytm
timeline

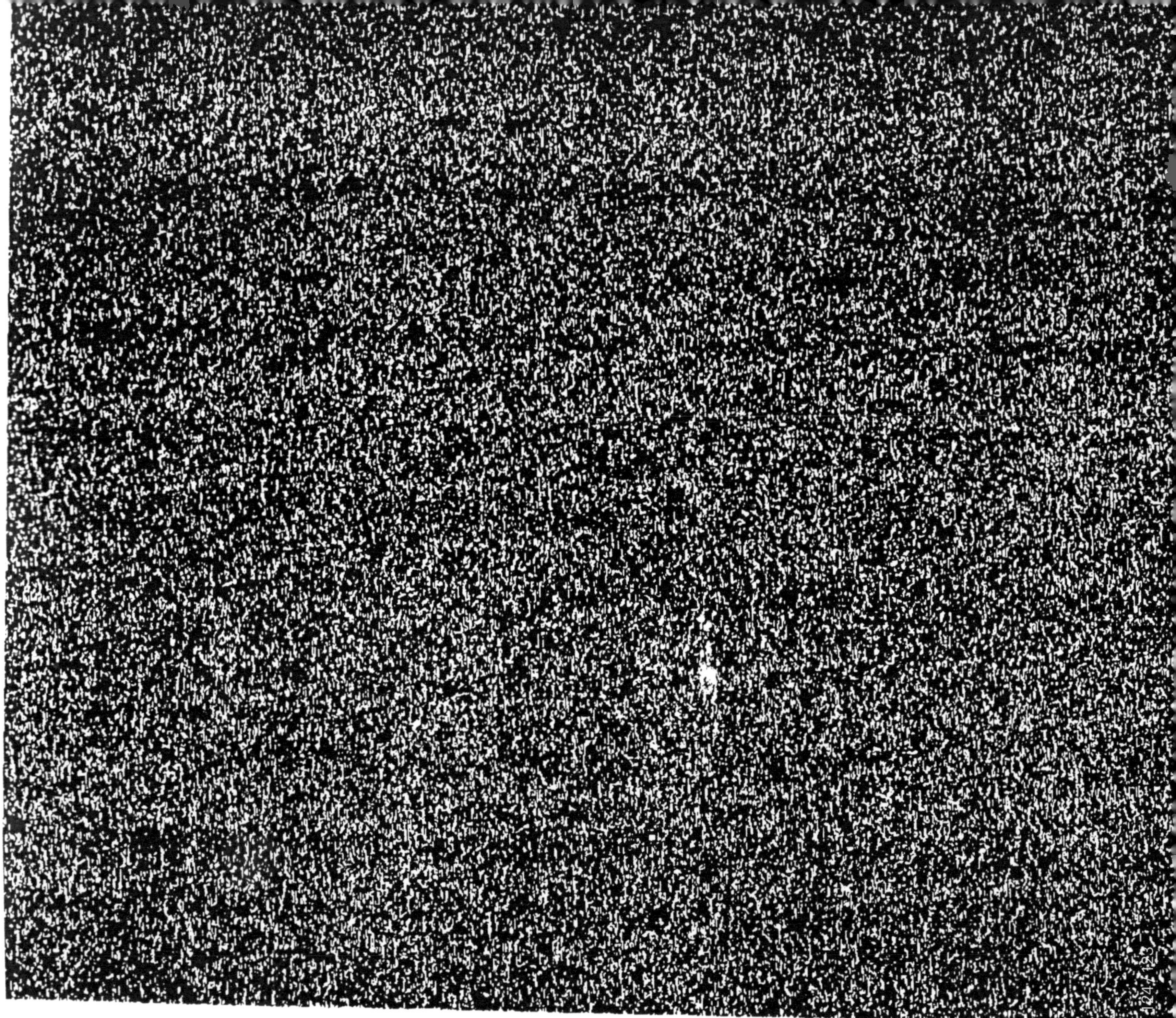

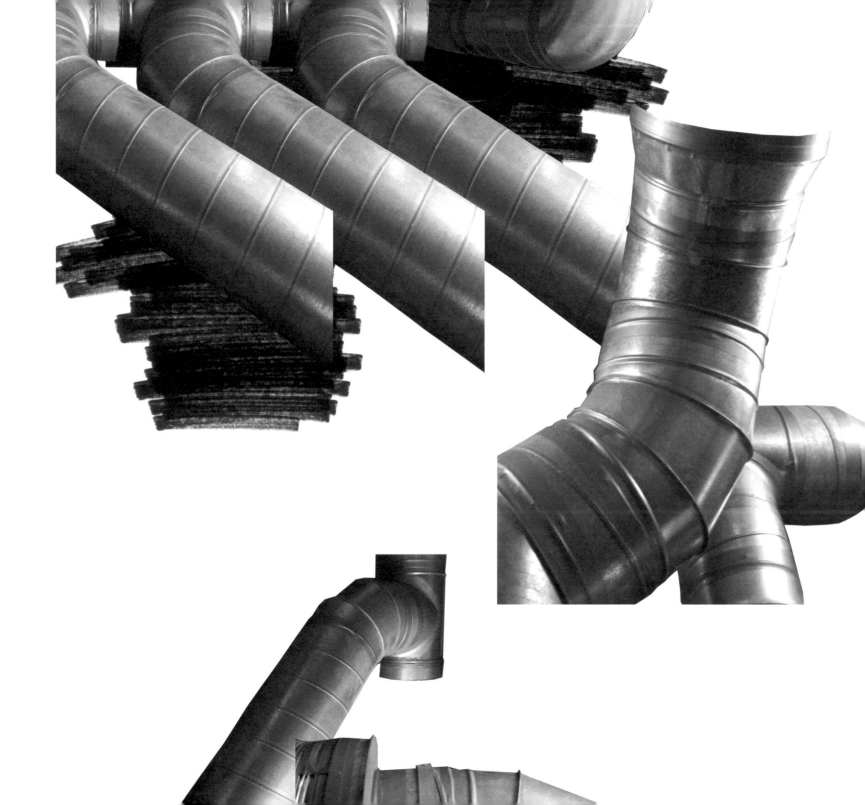

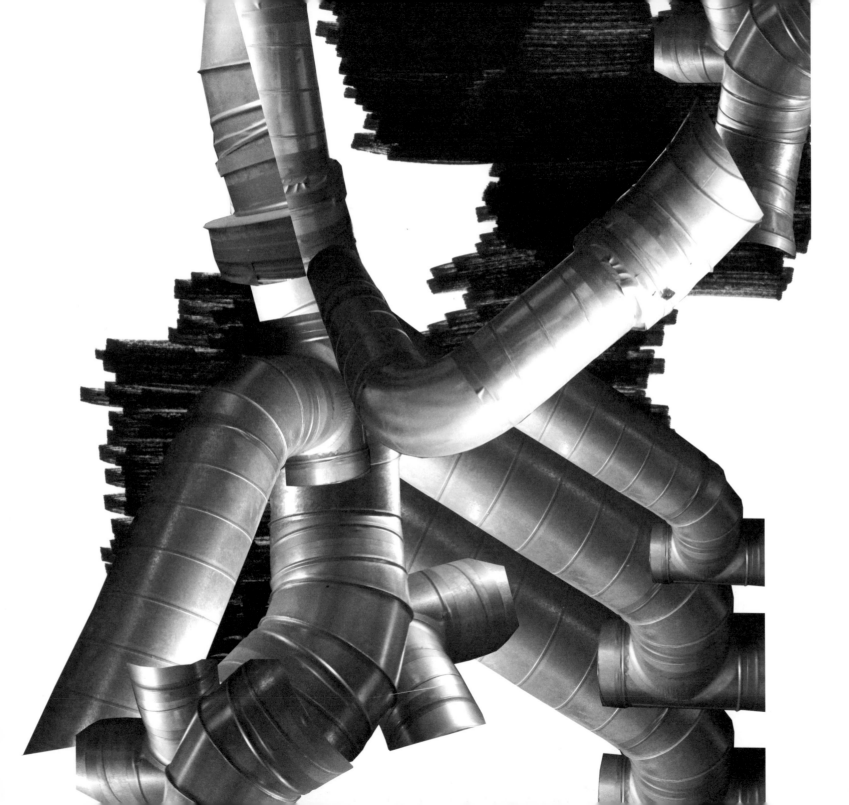

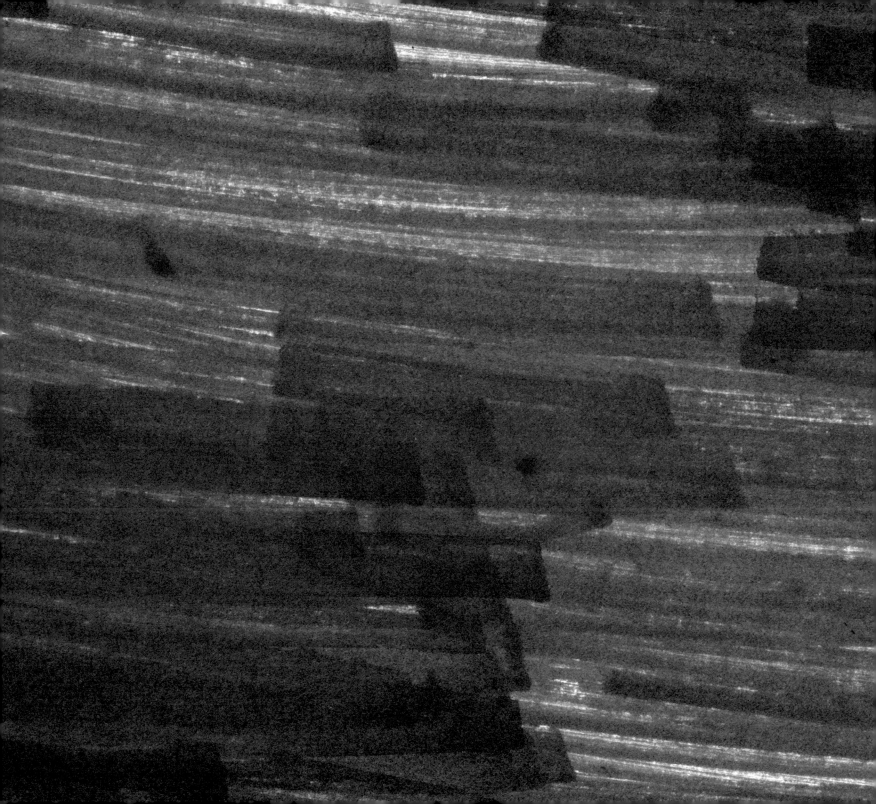

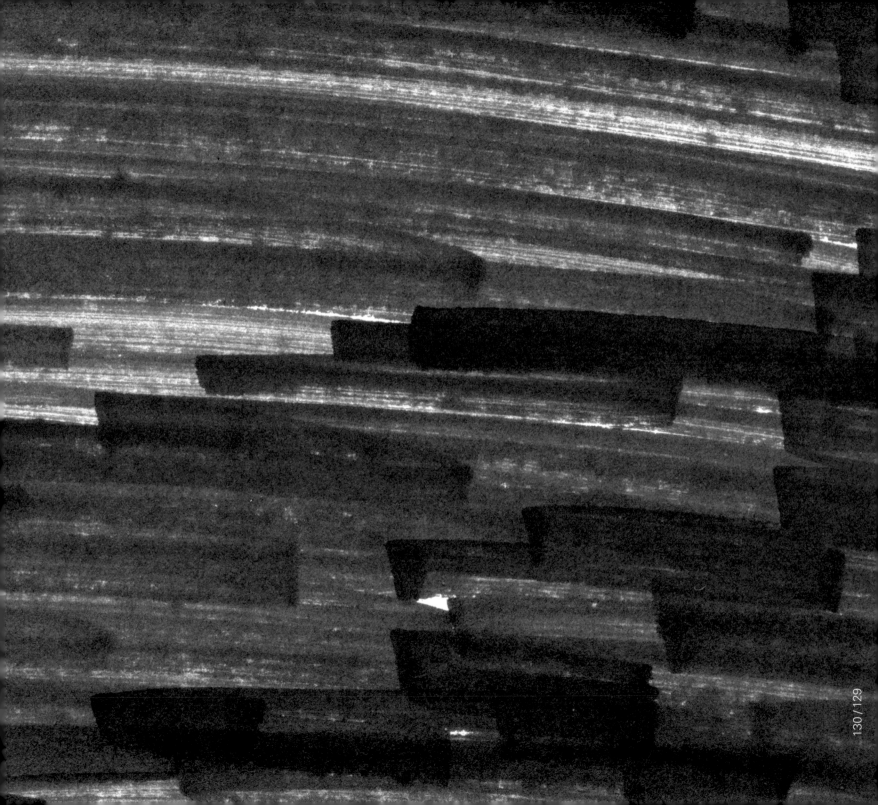

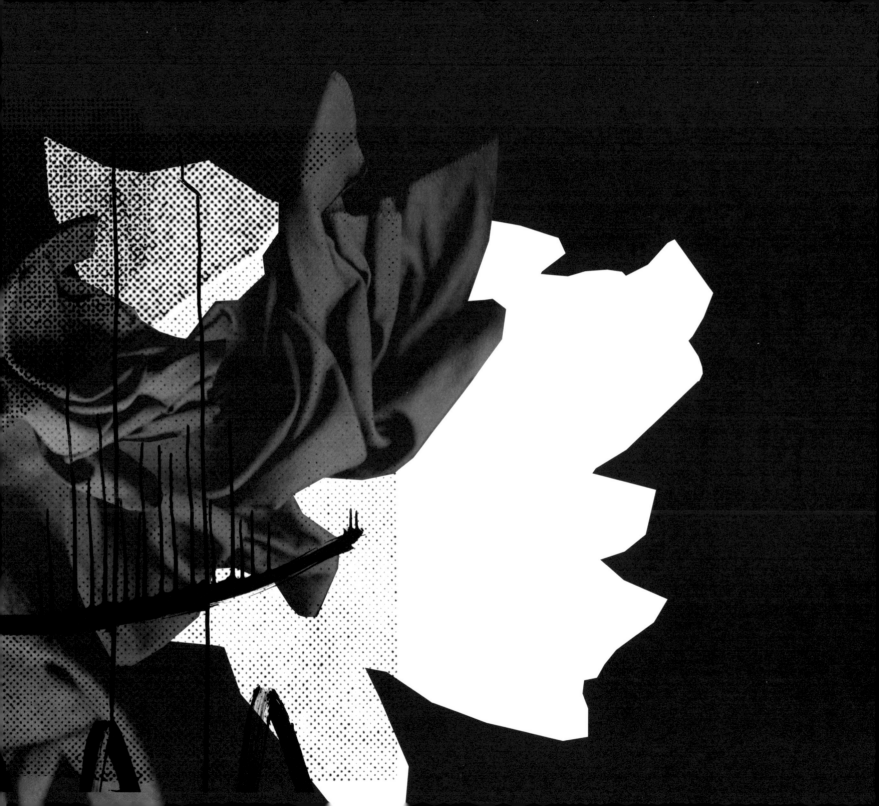

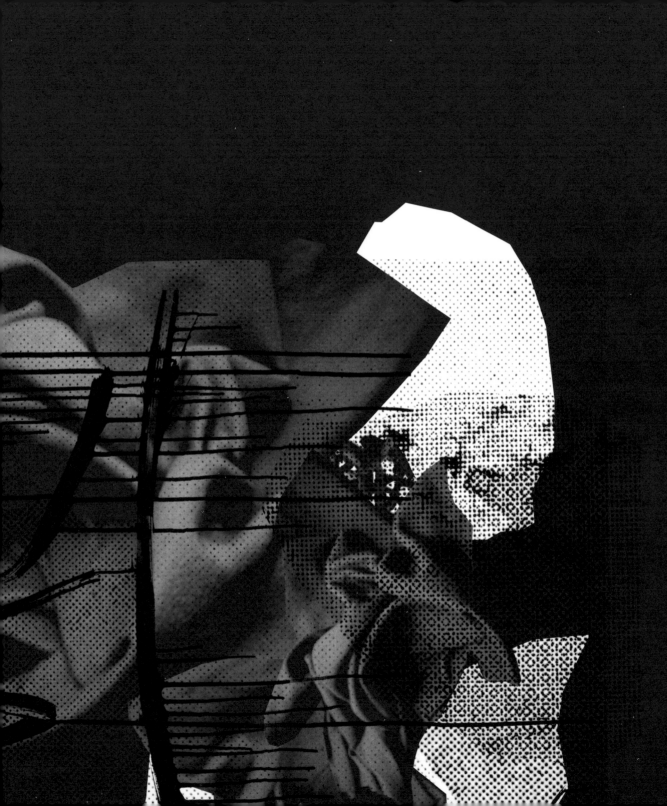

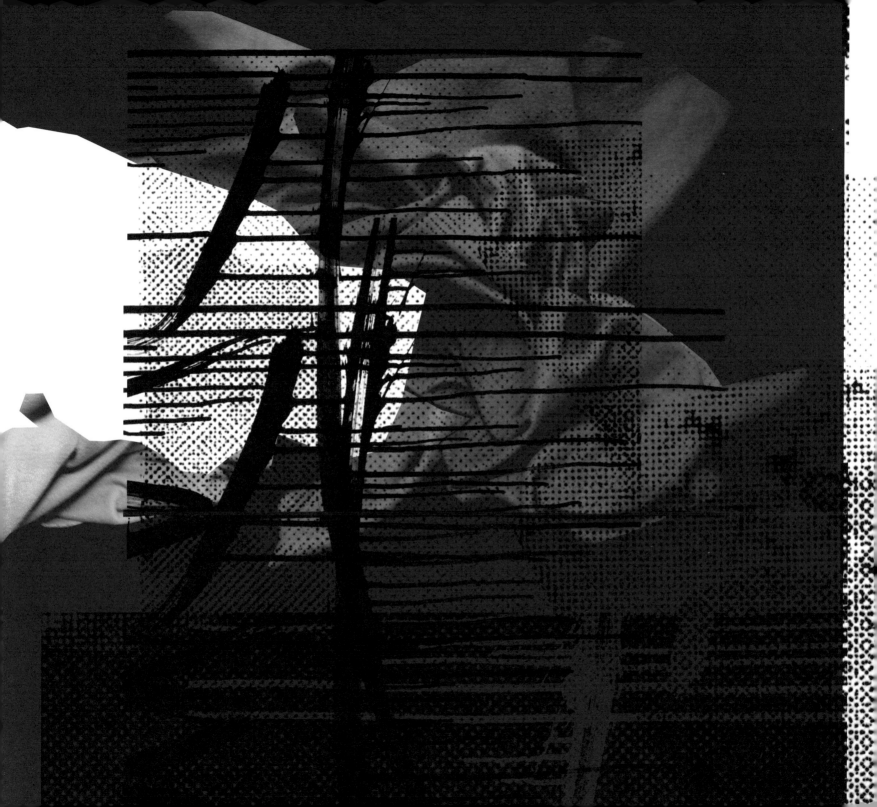

EVERY DAY LOOKS GOOD

ALIBI DAYS —

MORE OR LESS PRECISE
SUBSTITUTE FOR SILENCE

WHEN YOU ARE CONCENTRATING ON DRAMATIC / HISTORIC IDENTITY,
ALL YOUR OWN PROBLEMS DISAPPEAR — MOST PEOPLE DON'T WANT TO BE SHOT

DO YOU THINK THAT OLDER MEN
DISLIKE GIRLS WITH STRONG FACES?
BE MY WIFE

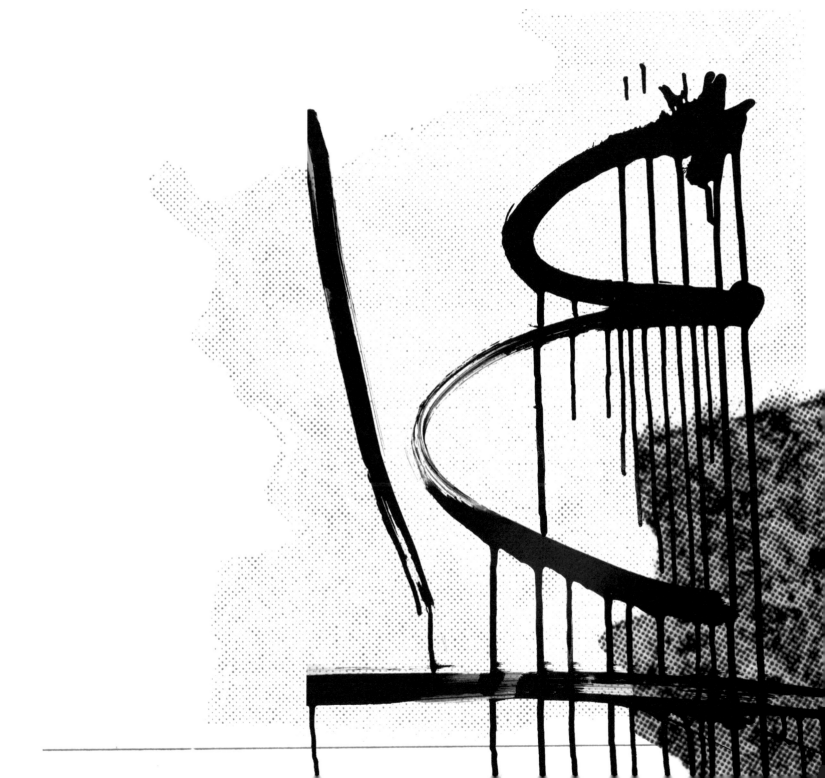

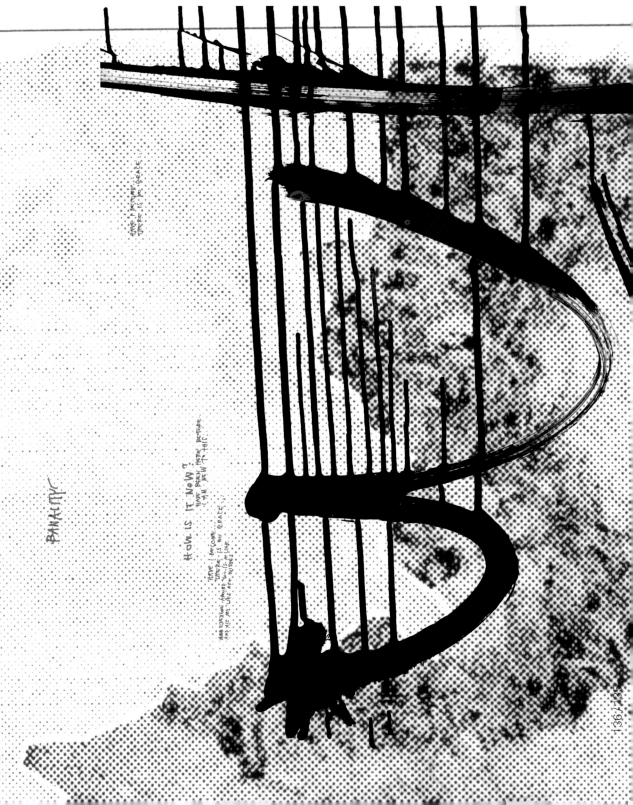

BANKSY

HOW IS IT NOW?
HAVE BEEN HERE BEFORE-
YEAH YEAH? IT THIS?

HAVE I BECOME
THERE IS NO SPACE.
SEE EVERYONE AROUND YOU IS IN SPACE.
AND YET MY LIFE ARE NUMBERS LINE

HAVE I BECOME
THERE IS NO SPACE-

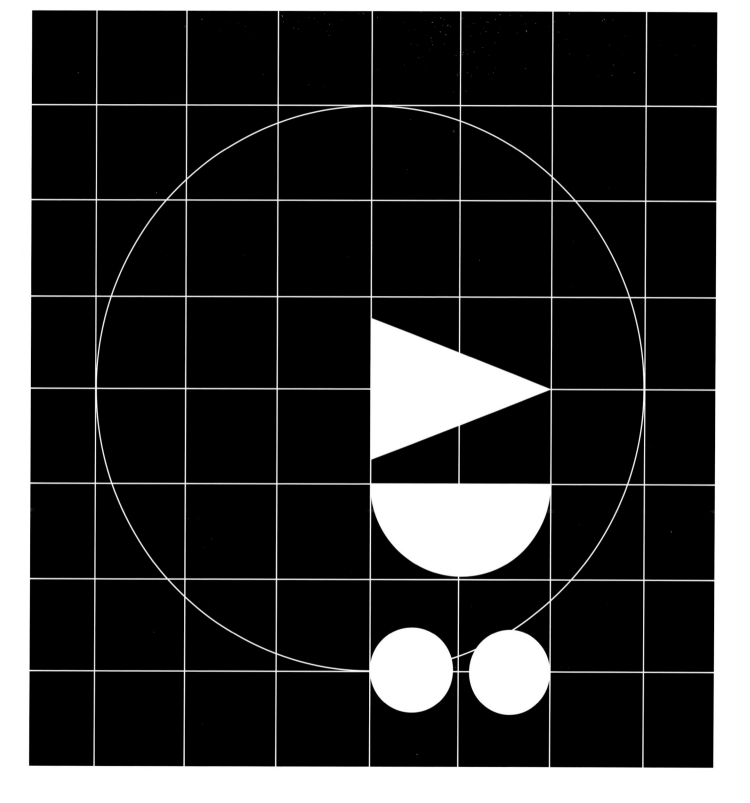

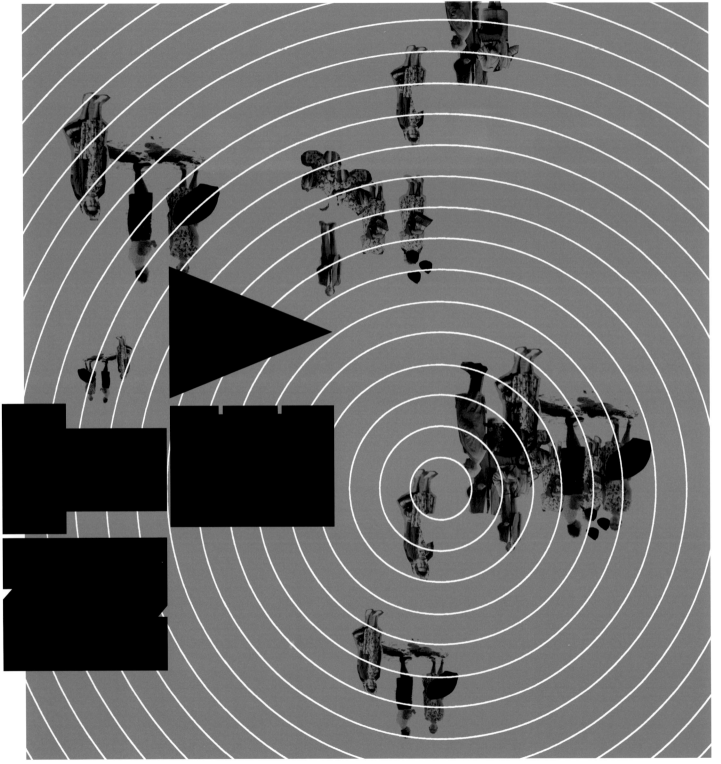

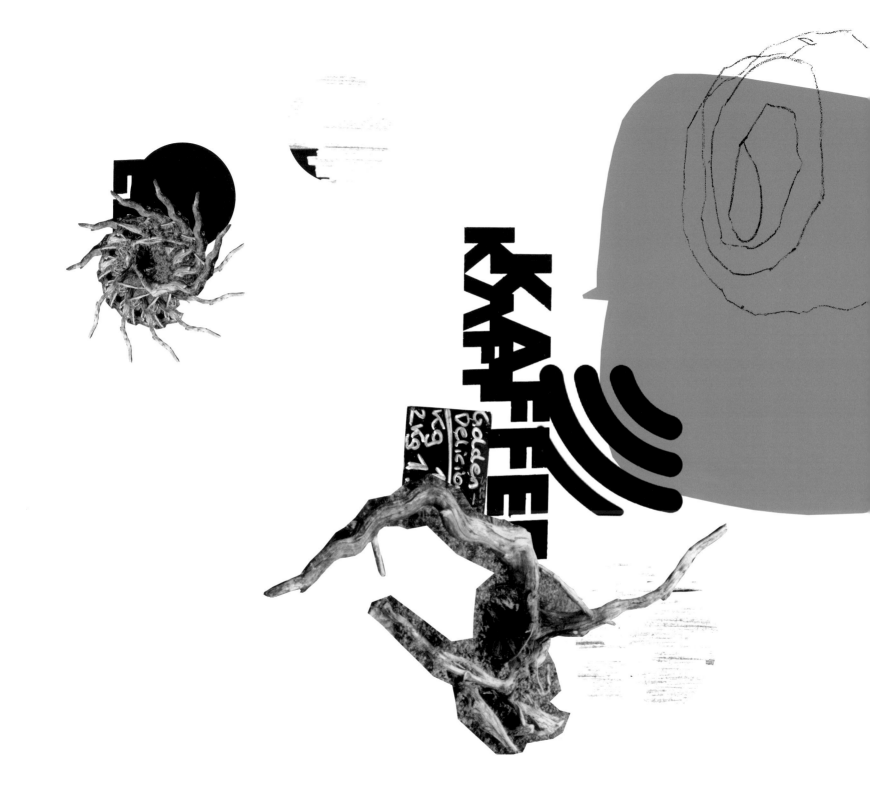

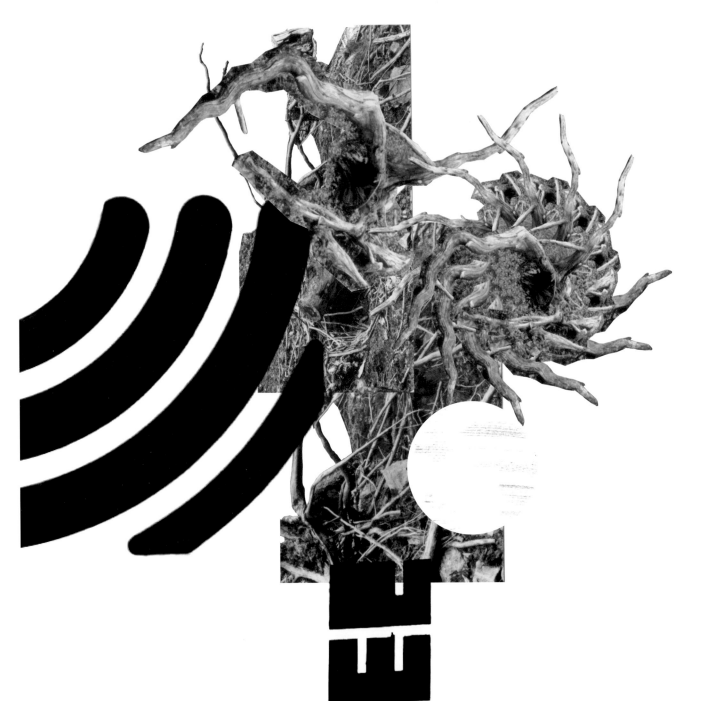

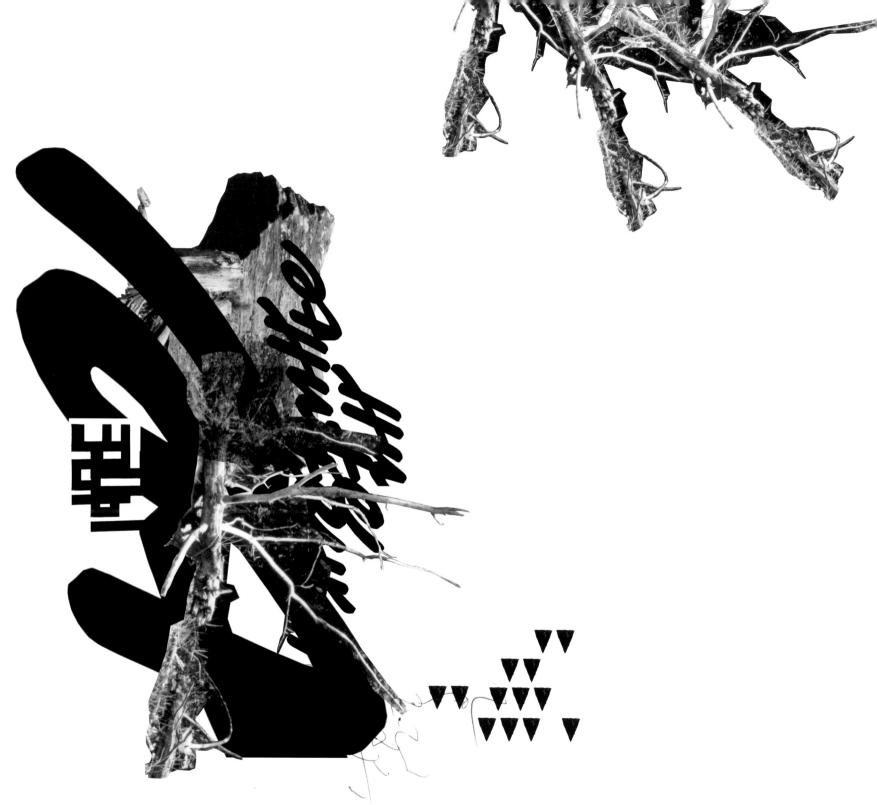

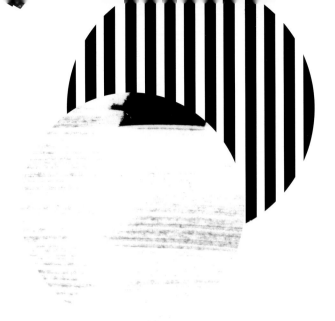

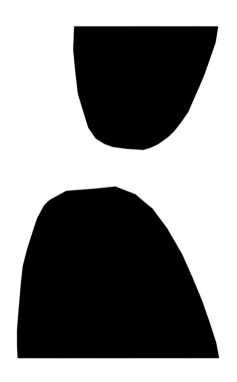

1/

2/

3/

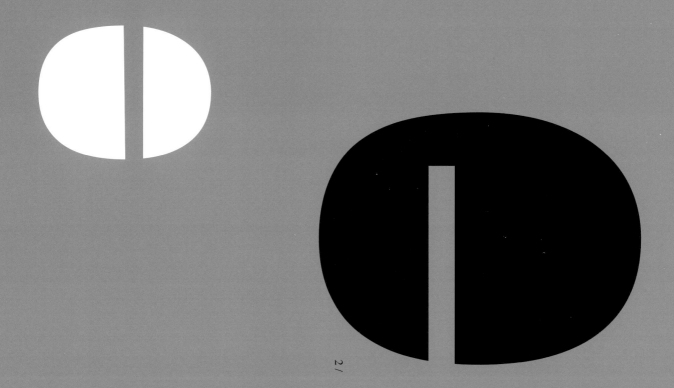

21

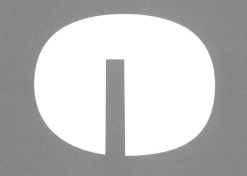

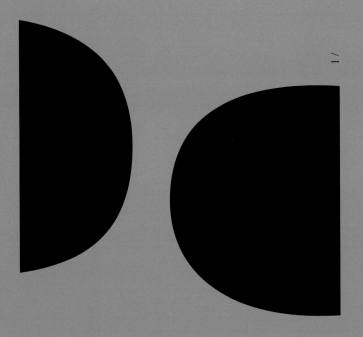

1/

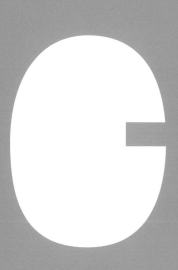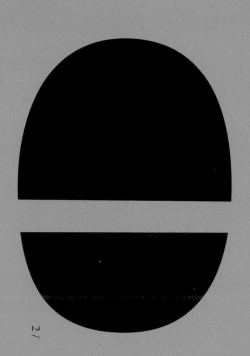

21

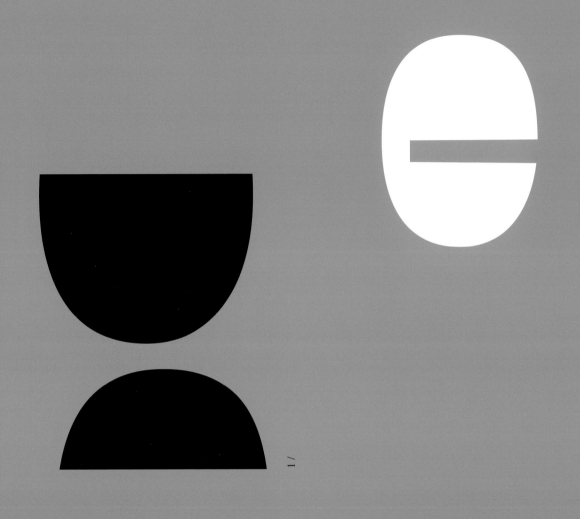

1/

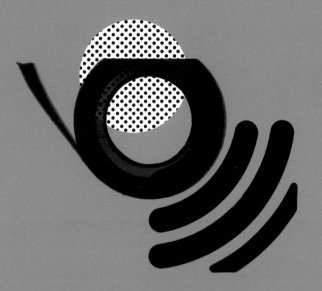

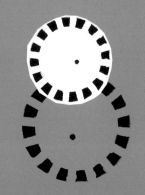

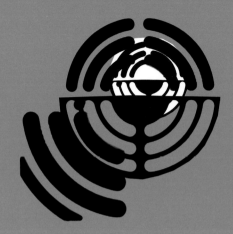

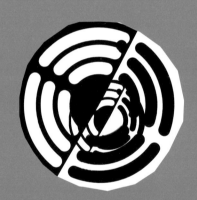

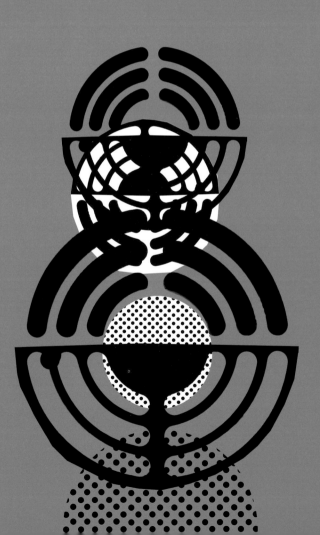

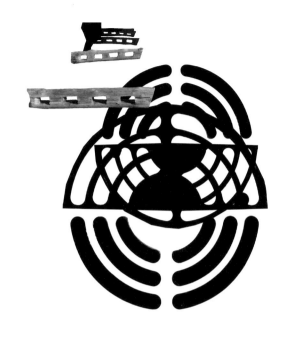

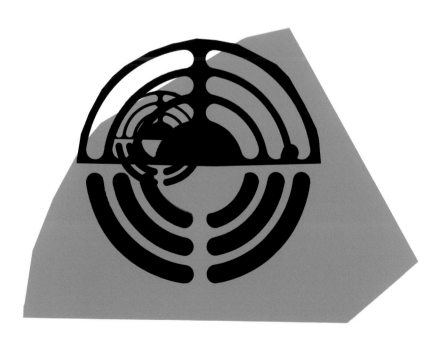

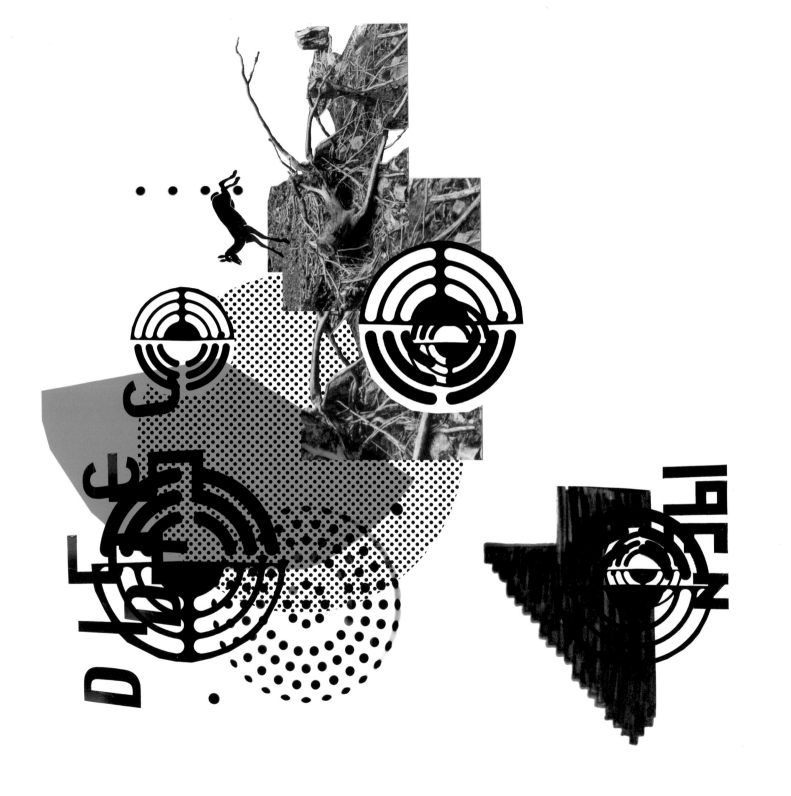

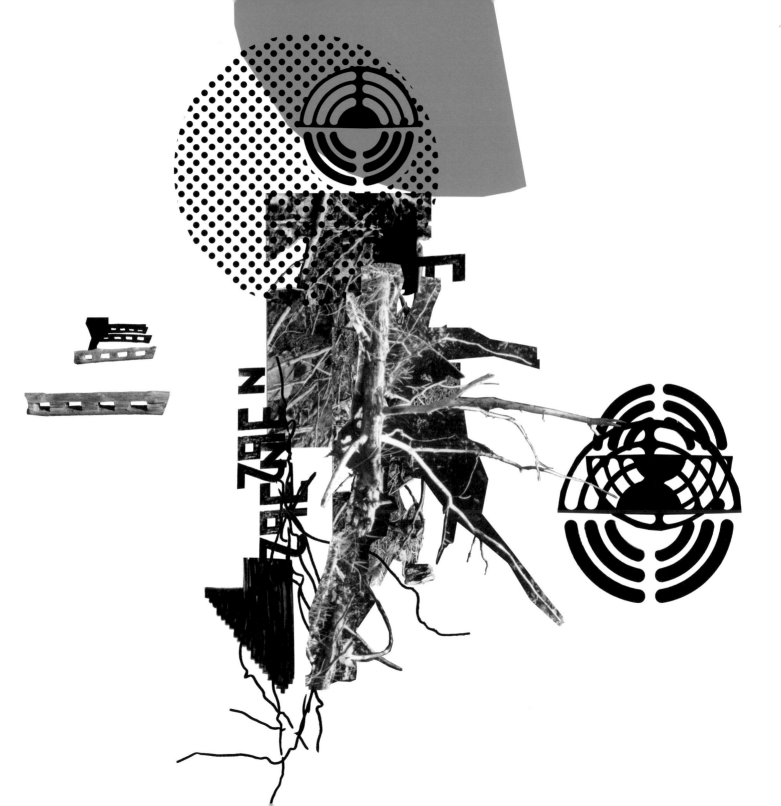

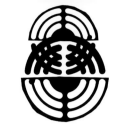

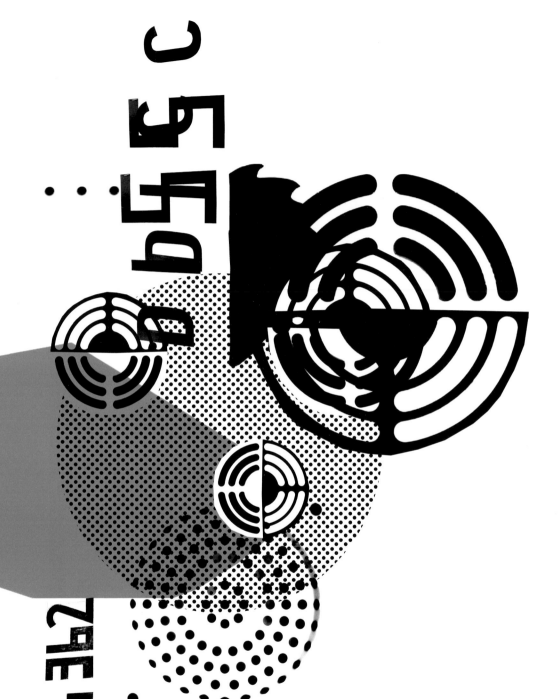

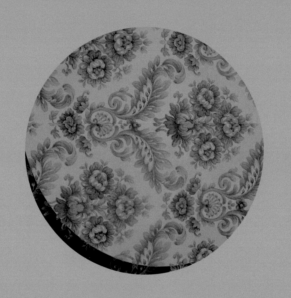

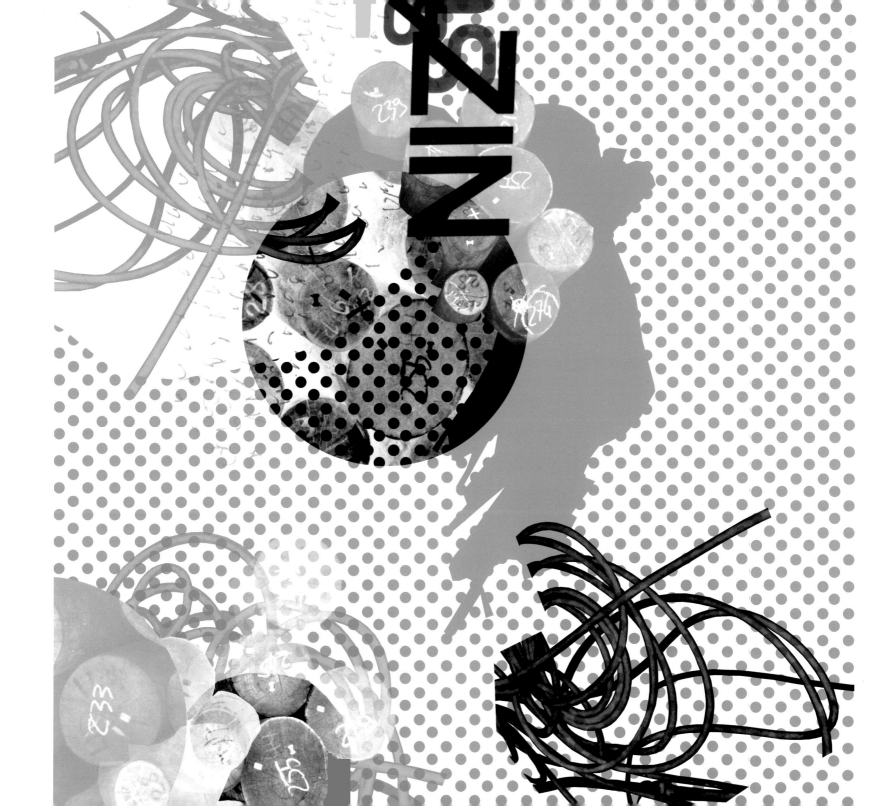

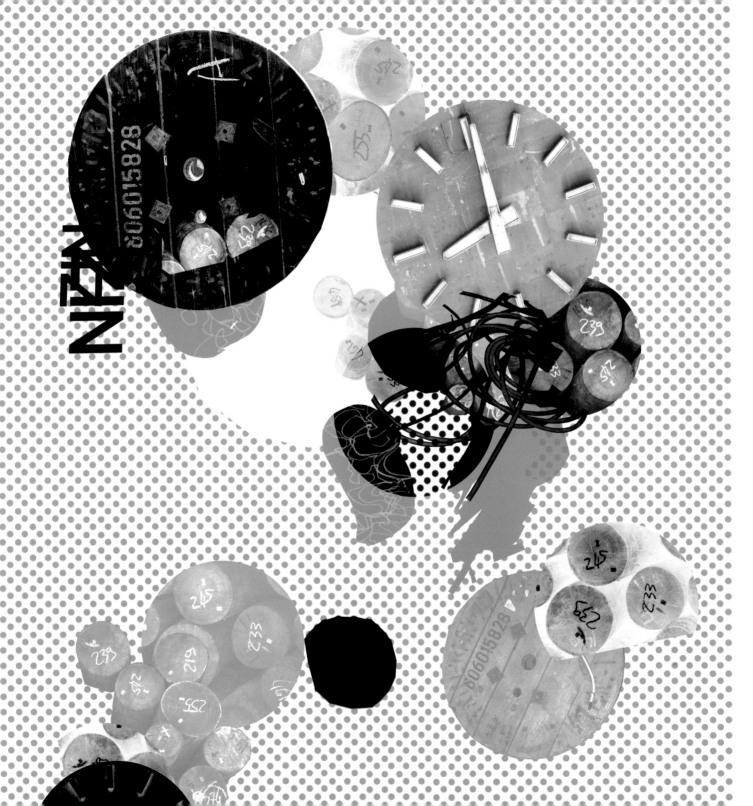

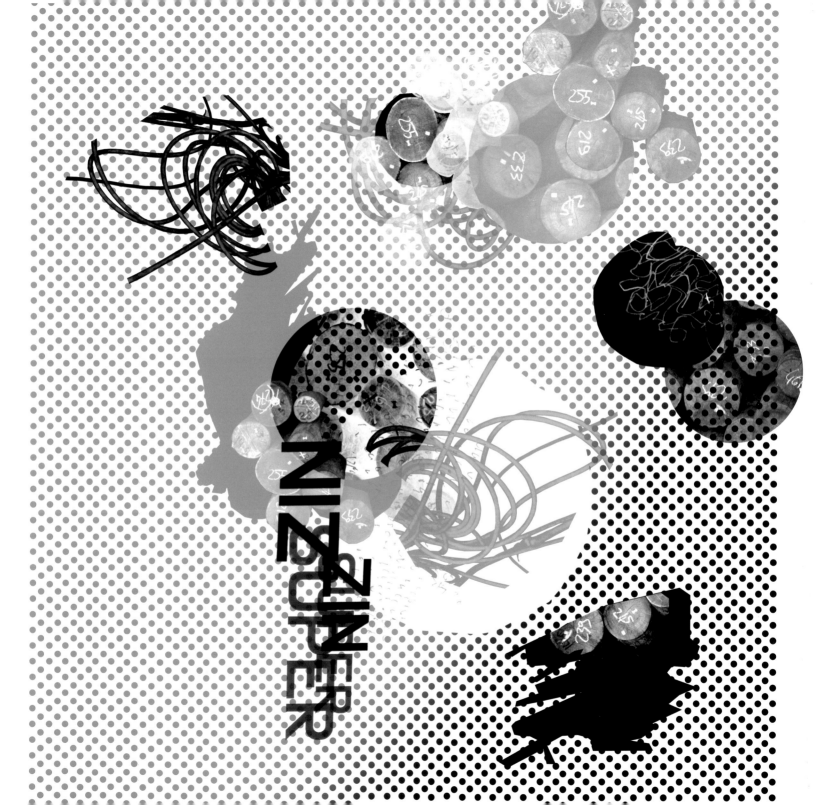

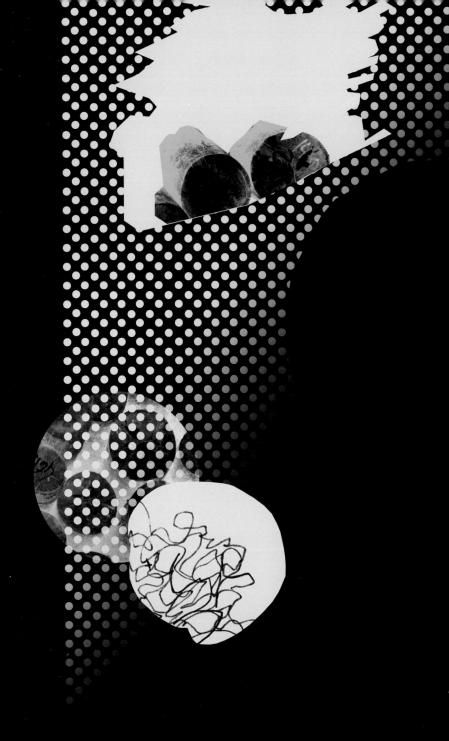
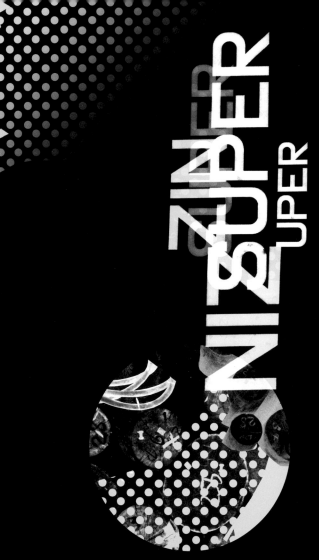
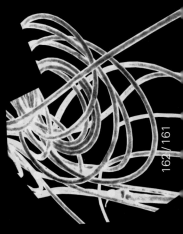

SUPER
UPER

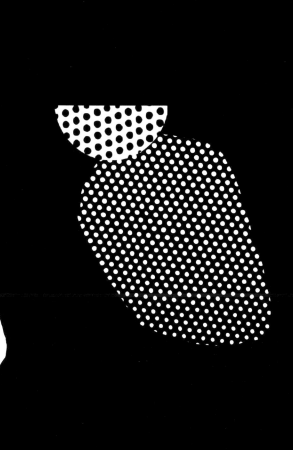

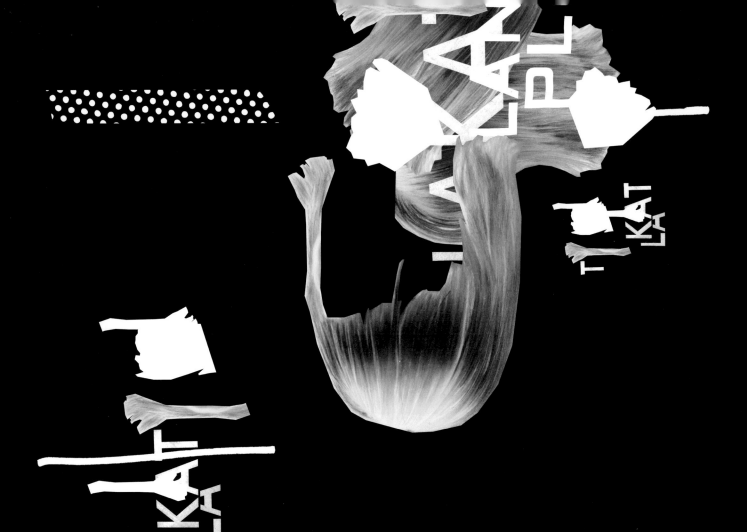

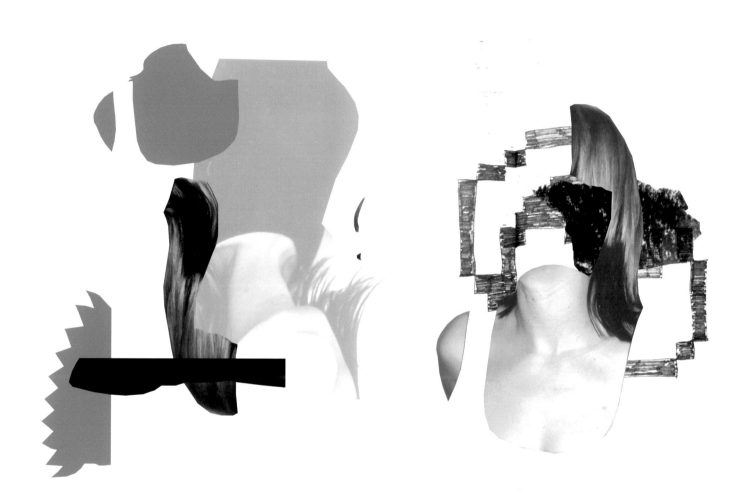

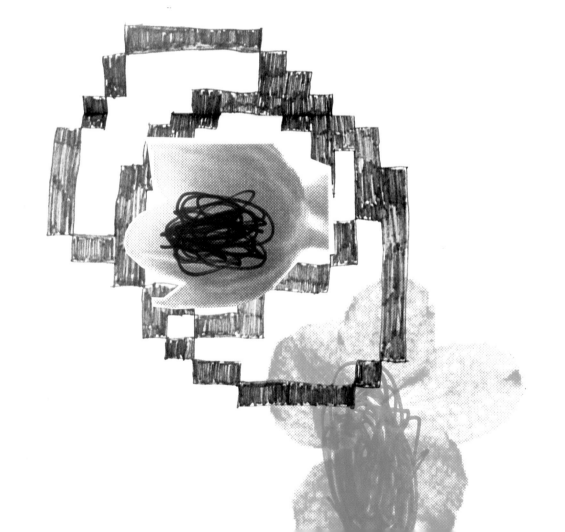

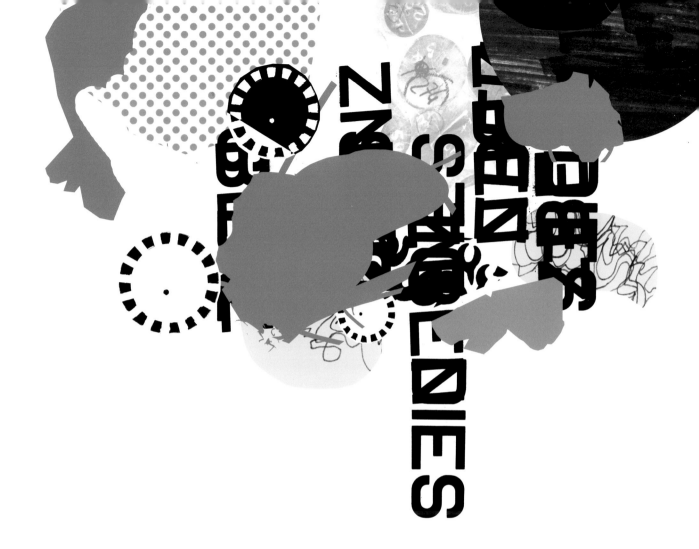

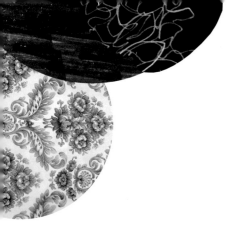

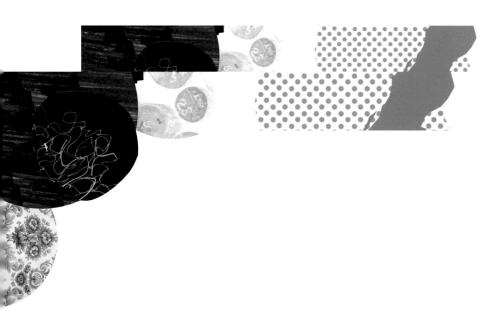

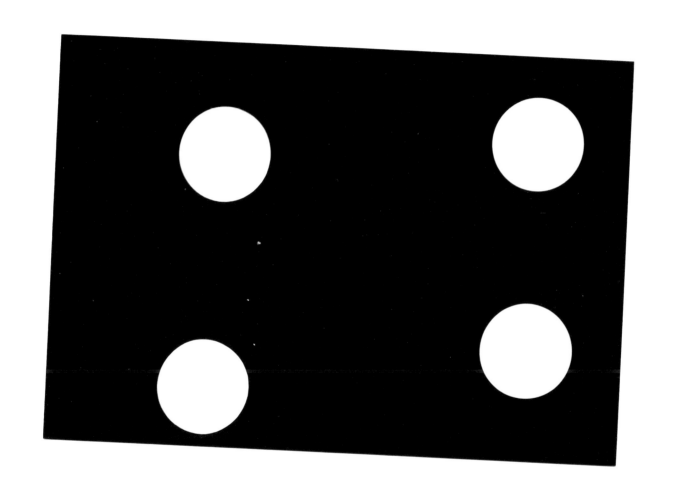

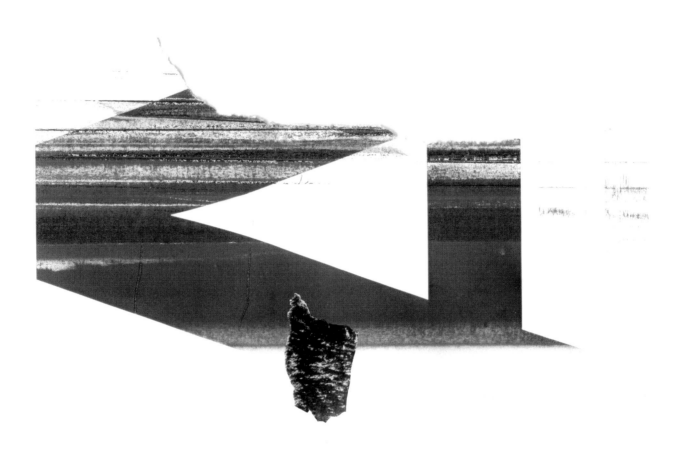

Drifting in this subliminal, nearly autistic metastate of awareness, being dusted, streaked, touched, or irradiated with impressions from the material that can either remain out of focus or make sense for unexplainable reasons, one keeps one's mind attentive and open to anything interesting, any influence or disturbance, ready to absorb it while playing memories backwards and forwards in an endless Ping-Pong game between the past and the present, the already learned and the new, reflecting upon and reconsidering all perceptions, picking out one of a multitude of realities. Depending on what one's attention appropriates, counterparts can be found in poetry, politics, the alien, and the familiar, and in fallacies and acts of encouragement. Calm and hysterical, easy and incomprehensible, coherent and continuous, the daily personal grind translates into a certain and therefore recognisable objectivity, unstable and ready for further processing.

Why, when things are broken, do they seem like more than when they're together? 19)

The images present themselves as transit areas comparable to waiting rooms, train stations, or airports where the observer strolls about. These are places that try neither to attract nor to take anything. Fragmental texts transcribed from real public areas provide visual hints that tend to demonstrate the presence of unexplored opaque meanings and provide textures able to show a possible approach to or determine a frame for the whole image. These texts are not reduced to catchphrases, but function as intermediate forms and stages of thoughts, indicating the presence of an additional layer of signs and symbols issuing from various contexts.

Modelling the modulations and oscillations of unorganized material is cultural work, which brings images into being. Every transmission of a message contains interferences, depending on the medium. One attempts to conceive of disturbances as not being distracting and troubling white noise, artefacts of compression, or printing raster, but as an interacting contribution of information – not as a malfunction of communication, but as irritating threads of dialogue winding across the stagnating proposals of mass culture. Repeated copying and transcription back and forth among the different media veils and partly destroys the identity of the medium of the basic material. But in this process, more than simply obscuring the medium, a possible situation is created whereby the images themselves become mixed with one another and with the surrounding world. Loss of detail and technological quality is gained in directness, grain, dynamics, pattern, and texture. By getting involved in the battle against a bored and boring consensus between producer und consumer, one is contributing to the collective consciousness and group memory.

Even what might be seen as primarily anti-social intervention can be integrated, taking effect as a corrective method applied in accordance with the prevalent thinking. The technique of visual montage sometimes causes a disconnection in the visual contiguity of the assembled forms. These interruptions in coherence can cause organisational tasks to stop the sequence of a storyline, thus demanding further considerations, redefining habits, or taking positions. Breaks in the order of events counter the formation of illusions and reveal additional conditions and states within the single elements and the entity as a whole.

A perfect, naturalistic replication of reality, the act of completing a collection, or an authentic preservation of stories with the intention of bringing back sentimental memories is neither desirous nor possible, the main aim being a shift from the sophisticated presentation of a final product to illuminating the path thoughts take that will possibly lead to the end result. By moving the place where things happen away from the obvious and immediately visible, every page seems to be an accumulation of fragments of further and deeper thoughts.

An arbitrary but not accidental access to the images is obtained by regarding any image or sequence with an unobstructed, untainted, and lucid view, detached and dissociated from personal wishes and intentions. In randomly opening this book, turning one's attention to the first form to appear, supplementing it with the next to capture the eye's attention, thus locking away a little fragment in passing that one associates with a thought, a memory, or any other kind of personal information gleaned from experiences stored away in one's mind, one establishes a personal relationship to the work, correlated according to one's background. Flicking through the pages until one's vision begins to blur, one stops, starts again, goes on, slowing down, accelerating, reconsidering, understanding, or rejecting. Turning to the next page or back to the previous one for more information, one adds input to the visual footage and, in case of dissatisfaction or doubt, at least experiences an undefined presentiment about the topic, issue, or expression. Very likely the person is touched in a positive way by the invitation and the hint to individually assemble meanings for him or herself. Meaning can therefore be defined as anti-totalitarian, anti-hierarchic, anti-monopolistic, non-linear, and non-arbitrary options for connections within the available material.

Text samples, individual letters, and parts of words are thrown in and generate additional dynamics capable of influencing the visual field. Impulses are exchanged and transmitted from one system to another, not necessarily with the aim of telling a story, but rather, to transport a possible interconnection of impulses. Such feedback serves to produce constant circulation in an infinite and diffuse system of differences like a semantic layer, interwoven with the visual forms. Cross-talks are raised at the intersections: Are semantically dead sentences – i.e., those that have been crossed out or are unreadable or ambiguous – still able to communicate something? Instead of being awed by elaborate melodies or contemplating many-voiced compositions that follow a linear path or a strict script, one can draw confidence from becoming involved and participating in a direct, and from the standpoint of logic, not entirely ascertainable process of understanding, which takes place inside the spectrum between the sensible fragility of field recordings and the flickering noise of construction machines.

18) Marshall McLuhan: Understanding Media: The Extensions of Man

An inquiry into the functionality of attention itself as directions for use might include browsing through the pages like children with a lookbook, all the while paying attention to the most insignificant details and finding and inventing new stories for the images that often differ from what the author had intended. Never knowing if he or she has given him or herself enough time to assimilate everything, the reader is like a dog wandering and snuffling about as it follows tracks or like someone who walks through a city not paying attention to the streets, preoccupied, and more distracted than focussed.

... is simply the fact that in the area of information movement, the main "work to be done" is actually the movement of information. The mere interrelating of people by selected information is now the principal source of wealth in the electric age. 18)

A non-representative presentation that includes uncommented situations, visual footnotes without principal text, an astonishing concurrence of facts which do not seem to belong together – images provoking short-circuits, offcuts, and waste, collisions evoking new perspectives, and cases of destruction marking decisive points – all provide departure points and frames encouraging the viewer to take a look at his or her own boundaries. Processed material worked up for distribution by the mass media, and as a consequence cleaned of irrelevant, ambiguous, and suggestive meanings – material which is repeatedly transformed and reintegrated into the different information flows – is as much a part of the analysis as raw and untreated material provided by nature and is handled in the same way, without distinction as to relevance, importance, or meaning.

When harmless-looking friends or friends of friends stopped by, I'd step out and tape and photograph them, and then I'd go back into my office and wait for somebody else to drop by. Now that I think back on it, I guess it was all the mechanical action that was the big thing for me at the Factory at the end of the sixties. I may have felt confused myself, but the sounds of phones and buzzers and camera shutters and flashbulb pops and the Moviola going ... – all those things were reassuring to me. I knew that work was going on, even if I didn't have any idea what the world would come to. 17)

In taking action, intervening, exploring in depth, and going on without complaint, one works to counteract the feelings of passive suffering, self-pity, and apathy by means of the personal activity of production: an active life, with work as the vehicle for infiltrating, revising, participating in social life even though the production process is a solitary experience. The results are never final, complete, or fixed and involve the individual recipient's existence, which gains integration into social life as a result of his or her interaction with the creator's work. Acceptance and refusal are uncontrollable external assessments that induce additional possibilities of interpretation – a strategy against the defensive techniques of differentiation. Decisions are taken not to clarify or persist in viewpoints or opinions, but to demonstrate an inherent desire to have them reviewed and screened, taking the risk of being mistaken, corrected, or opposed, with determined and precise conditions and horizons at the outset to be further developed and processed. Progress can not be attained directly, but only with an indirect approach.

In times of radical crisis everything depends on the individual who says no, who, acting out of the courageous impulses of human solitude, refuses to assent to a power that would be totalizing. 15)

An infinite flood of images is produced and reproduced on a daily basis, selected and distributed, attracting attention in a shrill and penetrating way, trying to overwrite and influence preceding visual inputs. The silence is suppressed by the insistent hullabaloo of exuberant parades and promising attractions. A rational and intellectual categorisation and a rigorous scientific analysis alone are not on a level to be able to gain an overview and perceive the complex spectrum that would probably be attainable in a sleepwalk-like process of voluntary observation, which seems to be able to intuitively read and decode silence as well as it can loud chaos. However, a subject becomes all the more enigmatic, the more interesting and rich the content, the more exactly and intensely one devotes oneself to it, and the more time one spends with it and delves into it.

14)
Banana Yoshimoto: *Amrita* (trans.
Russell F. Wasden)

Collecting moments, objects, events, concepts, thoughts, and views in order to exchange life experiences presents the viewer with a restrained invitation to reflect and synchronise. The initial goal is not even to incite participation in any active or conscious way, as finding a starting point for taking action is arduous and requires courage. To this purpose, those half-aware moments and routines can be used when thoughts tend to stray into a nearly automatic type of orbiting, when one can benefit from the pauses and lack of concentration, imperceptibly touched and absorbed by the magnetic field of something unknown. Dealing with semi-conscious thoughts and suddenly noticing that the mind is occupied with something located in the field of perception, the viewer most likely finds him or herself involved, with spontaneous, meandering thoughts shaping themselves out of this semi-obvious, unconscious thinking process that happens uncontrollably and continually.

I suppose that was the reason I always thought about the meaning of life as well. Moreover, I've never felt comfortable sharing my thoughts on the subject; then again, regardless of how long I try to stay quiet, the next thing I know I'm suddenly babbling what I think to others. Whenever I talk to people about it, it doesn't matter if they agree or not. If we did agree it would be useless. Every thing important would just disappear in succession, one thing right after another, starting from one end and moving to the next. In the end they'd be completely gone, only a silhouette remaining. Even then I would feel a certain sense of comfort—or at least that's how I feel about it now. 14)

16)
Angela Bulloch: *Art Now 2*

The works often continue to evolve after they have been realised, simply by the fact that they are conceived with an element of change, or an inherent potential for some kind of shift to occur. 16)

Anything definite would not be interesting enough to be shown because of its obvious and static nature. The images concentrate on what is variable. Working with existing material familiar to both viewer and creator eases acceptance by instituting a neutral starting position and dissolving preset structures of thinking through a transparent reorganisation: repetition holds an element of displacement and a mutation of quality. The necessity to avoid taking something for granted is essential in order to gain a deeper understanding. Nothing is self-evident: everything may also be different. Each detail contains various inherent possibilities of existence that are able to appear at any given time in completely divergent ways and can propel things forward.

The content presented can be amplified and enlarged when each individual recipient adds a particular moment of personal reality by reflecting upon and criticising the images: not demarcating and differentiating one specific life, but conceiving a system of interdependent microcosms that are only viable within a community – a single self, multiplied a million times, embedded in an abstract open space where the public and the private collide. Perhaps the appropriate form of expression is not phrased, written text, but comparable to the floating nuances of spoken language: patchy, bumpy, and economically not as efficient as direct communication because of having too little of the simplification and standardisation that facilitates a fast and impeccable data transaction. But actually, the imperfect cataloguing, the repetitions with the unexpected imprecision, and the returning again and again to the same issues that are all involved in speech keep the attention level of the viewer high and the relevant things can instead be said and shown in passing: not indoctrination, but just a sort of respectful (re)creating of remembrances, a relationship of trust between the possibly dissenting parties of creator and viewer.

The two-dimensional flatness of the images produces the effect that formal visual decisions gain power by appropriating the space left by the absence of any apparent physical structure. The rawness and imperfection of the images stimulates the freedom for other images and, as a consequence, for the viewer as well to dock or attack at the borders. The process of research is reflected in seemingly improvised, imaginary situation aesthetics. Analogue set-pieces are edited with digital technologies and prepared for distribution via channels for mass media. The speed of production consequently reflects the creator's participation in a fast-moving external world. Recycling visual elements within the images of a book, sometimes returning to already sorted out material, implies an anti-consumeristic, anti-corporate statement. Neglecting technical virtuosity outlines a counterplot to the increasing sophistication and glitziness of the zeitgeist.

From a formal point of view, a book's ability to bring incoherent single images into a sequence makes it a suitable medium for the present concept. Furthermore, a book's intimacy manifests itself in the individual's solitary experience of reading or viewing, with the inherent possibility for the viewer to go at his or her own pace (unlike with a film), with the option of interrupting or disconnecting, interpreting, or actively appropriating its pre-structured content. A book as a haptic object that allows for the use of the learned and established, nonexclusive, and ancient metaphors of navigation seems to ease understanding, in contrast to purely virtual data. The enhanced non-linear concept and method a book provides should also be able to provide assistance in an orientation to the digital world, where diverse, non-hierarchical and rhizoidal forms of displaying and structuring content are developed.

A restricted and economic use of the tools facilitates articulateness and supports consciousness and sustainability, whereas spending a considerable part of a budget on the printing production in order to create impressive glossy effects to make the content seem more interesting and important is common practice.

For me voluntary memory, which is, above all, memory of the intellect and of the eyes, gives us only the appearance, not the reality, of the past. But when a smell or a taste, rediscovered in totally different circumstances, reveals the past for us, in spite of ourselves, we feel how different this past is from what we thought we remembered, and what our voluntary memory painted for us, like bad painters who have their colours but no truth. 12)

To commit basic material to memory requires a codification accomplished by a translation into symbols that can be interpreted by an audience. The subjective results of observation are translated in intersubjective relationships. A book liaises the creator's memory with the viewer like a container of thoughts that can be accessed – a discursive system at everyone's disposal. The viewer discerns the creator's observations in an observation of secondary order, which is a loaded and stylised form of culture. If no echo or immanent re-orientation can be established by the viewer through focussing his or her attention in a second look on his or her own manner of observation, the work ends by not going beyond absolutism or contemplation. Distances are reduced – not only between viewer and creator, but also between the viewer and himself – in a constant scrutiny of the prevailing circumstances and parameters.

The preparation and evaluation of the material by any given person are conceptual means of generating an abstract communicative and discursive level of never-apodictic statements suspended in an intermediate phase of temporary awareness and control that allows one to approach the outside world, become stimulated, and face emerging problems. It is important to be able to let go in a context of involvement without entirely losing one's own identity. The non-organic development processes of selection and reflection follow intuitive criteria and strategies of trial and error, repetition, established rituals, insistence, and review throughout. A specific, concrete presence is lifted out from the uniformity of the organic material and the conditions of life through the work of perception in a transaction from subconscious to conscious and an internalisation of the external occurrences. Volatile moments are equilibrated and valued within a phenomenological system of comparison.

13)
Roland Barthes: *The Eiffel Tower and Other Mythologies* (trans. Richard Howard)

<u>The perfect legibility of the scene, its formulation dispenses us from receiving the image in all its scandal; reduced to the state of pure language, the photograph does not disorganize us.</u> 13)

In tilling the vast fields of possibilities and discovering options to be transformed into reality by the viewer in an active and selective (creative) process, a continually challenging context of relationships within the material, between the material and the perceived, and within the memory sharpens the power and competence of judgement. The recipient is asked not only to assent, but to add meaning in the form of a personal opinion, thus performing a self-determinative and emancipating act in the tradition of humanism

Taking apart and classifying the individual parts implies dissolving a linear character in favour of an abstraction to the point that a generic readability shines through from behind – suspended, simultaneously both figurative and abstract, with an implicit tension between detailed views and roughly rendered abstract fragments. Connotative visual codes allow for various interpretations. Multi-layered variety introduces permissive points of view. The images act as a request for a reaction on the part of the recipient, cross-referencing plural entities able to formulate, synchronise, and reorient points of understanding.

An interactive relationship with a recipient, who enriches and combines the proposed with additional expressions and knowledge, is set up that generates in that recipient a curiosity for stories aside from his or her own. This is the inquiring spirit of research, the primary aim of which is not optimisation and efficiency, but a feeling of participation in and affiliation to the world and consequently a sense of embeddedness and confidence.

Exposed and shared cognitive routines are able to establish moments of discourse between sender and receiver: both parties tend to project personal opinions and life experiences onto the recorded images and to add from their personal backgrounds what in reality is missing. Trying to take advantage of this generates new information and consequent reconsiderations by prompting the collaboration of the viewer, who then explores and turns the material around in such a way that something else other than that intended by the author may also appear. Equivocal interference appears lively and vital. The immobile printed image serves as a nodal point for the variety of possible interpretations and implicit meanings. Bridging and creative combining enables thinking and therefore brings the main topic and focus of aesthetics into a position of dealing with questions not of taste, but of ethics and relations.

[...] the daily routine mix together with thoughts and reflections on how they appear in the images. Does one lose sight of where one's own thoughts end and external influences begin when immersing oneself in the surrounding atmosphere of the banal and seemingly irrelevant and then rearranging the individual pieces? How much information can be processed before everything breaks down in chaos? Can observation and analysis of the manner of absorbing information reveal anything about the perception process itself? Can uncertain results establish reliable communicational threads? This method is a rejection of the obstinate position of always wanting to invent something new, instead shifting to an attitude encompassing a willingness to listen, as well as humility and respect. Tangible, comprehensible, and easily accessible (democratic) starting points are preferred to brilliantly scintillating fireworks of ideas. The effort to come up with dazzling ideas is channelled by perceiving the surrounding environment as it presents itself: a concept of reality instead of originality. X-raying the material, and thereby the working process, brings with it the demystification of the aura of superiority surrounding the production of design and art. Not distinctive or unique features or particularities, but commonplace and plain details establish the basis for interaction and connections and unveil the rules. A documental character is established over one of empathy and sentimentality, with the aim of inspecting the conditions and constructions of the material as to type and quality without the influence of too obvious self-referential data or mandatory storylines, conscious of the impossibility of completely eliminating a subjective point of view.

Evaluating and gauging the great diversity of shapes, forms, signs, and structural schemes in the world fosters an interest in the oscillations between the systematics of these things, both inwardly and outwardly. Maintaining a certain tranquillity and distance is necessary in order to make an observation while delineating the single aspects in a candid way, which means without referring to the private sensitivities of a diary and by restricting oneself to presenting an altered reality through a structuration limited by personal possibilities and capabilities. The necessary conditions for observation to be established involve not placing oneself too much under pressure, not thinking too hard, not expecting anything or concentrating on the results, and not getting hysterical under the onslaught of impulses. Becoming attuned to this state of being in self-orbit without self-absorption, surrendering in the face of the material with great ease, and relinquishing self-control without fear of getting lost is certainly a very difficult operation.

One must maintain a certain distance to what is evident and overtly obvious, both of which never bear fruit, while seeking an accurate description in travelling the vague landscape of different levels of interpretation and understanding. Further, one must refrain from indulging in personal psychological conflicts in concentrating on an "objective" content, for thinking about oneself ends in itself and in attempts to put one's actions and decisions into the limelight, thereby embellishing them with sentimental and ingratiating approaches towards the potential audience and with self-exposing explanations or excuses for the disagreeable inconveniences of life. The more one is absorbed by the need to reveal personal emotions and to inflict them upon others in a frontally aggressive way, the less efficacious and sustainable are one's actions, for they provoke a certain degree of distance and feelings of revulsion.

<u>It is not the event wanting to be understood, but the pictures asking for counter-images, a film script, the concept for a montage that has taken hold of us.</u> 11)

8)
Banana Yoshimoto: *Amrita* (trans.
Russell F. Wasden)

9)
Rolf Dieter Brinkmann: *Der Film in
Worten* [Film in Words] (trans. E.
Nosowa)

10)
Hal Foster (trans. E. Nosowa)

Every so often there are times when I have a clear understanding of my surroundings, and oddly enough, everything was perfectly aligned that night. 8)

What happens to someone might happen to anyone else as well: Organising a predefined period of time into systematic structures that operate within a certain cultural pattern makes room for both abstract pro-cesses and concrete objects and events when one is observing, paying attention, sighting, collecting information and data, profiling, recording, documenting, archiving, researching, quoting, listing, denominating, cataloguing, preserving, scanning, transcribing, combining, comparing, referring, formulating, mapping, refining, simulating, criticizing, contrasting, analysing, standardising, selecting, distorting, generalising, translating, taking minutes, writing a report, or putting together a presentation.

When irritation occurs, the familiar, long inscrutable because of what it is, suddenly becomes clear – just for a moment. 9)

An occurrence only receives its validity when it has been recoded through another one. 10)

As one squints in the bright light of the vast material without becoming overly agitated or dramatic, aspiring to sober research into perception, memorisation, tradition, and communication, structure and significance are provided through an analytical process that avoids narrative ornaments and excited, overly emotional approaches. A paradoxical clarification removes continuities as one persistently carries out new examinations and creates new combinations, dissolving the apparently fixed identities and temporary ordering of things one usually relies on to classify and deemphasise the breaks and to simulate the continuities that occur in the course of life.

One attempts to find parameters and poles that both delineate one's own personal life reality and aid in finding a direct and open access to the world and an adequate form of description: simple and multi-faceted, instable and flexible, discrete and without agitation, basic and complex, private and public, present and scattered, profound and superficial; necessary, possible, evident and inquiring; implacable and compromising, strange and familiar; passionate, sluggish, confused, subtle, absurd, probable, repetitive, ascetic, and immoderate. Whether reserved, delicate, spontaneous, weak, self-evident, or incomprehensible; attractive or ugly, frightening or desiring, spontaneous or constructed; intimate, coordinated, or solitary; illusive or delusive, wonderfully logical or absurd, subtle or violent; conflicting, undogmatic, incomprehensible, mediocre, sublime, banal, disorientated, or unpredictable – every entity consists of a successive, ever-changing combination of individual elements.

likely differences in meaning of the individual textual and pictorial parts, are not only permitted, but deliberately provoked: a melting pot of positions for argument, dialogues, discussions, spontaneous contradictions, moments of confusion, perspectives, flashes of thought, rituals, commonplaces, stereotypes, interruptions, deviations, fluctuations, dynamics, balances, contacts, and relationships.

The more things happen, the more they speed up. Providing for all contingencies is just as impossible as it is desired: nothing can be definitely excluded; and even apparently incorrect, faulty, opaque, or incomplete information contains concrete possibilities. Immoderate input simultaneously evokes the feeling of an immeasurable void.

5)
Friedrich Nietzsche

In the case of everything's being perfect, we are accustomed to abstaining from asking how it became so. We rejoice in the present fact as though it had come out of the ground by magic. 5)

We must learn to wonder and to listen everywhere to the inevitable and suggestive expressions of the surrounding world, curious, open, and willing to let interchanges happen, prepared to receive the information. However, we should neither emotionalise, celebrate, or palliate the boredom of common everyday life, nor should we exchange it for a utopian escapism or create a stagey and pitiable artificial loftiness in an exaggeration of the banal.

On the other hand, brilliant ideas and flashy slogans of style superimpose themselves on reality as formal alibis and context-refusing, self-contained mystifications, sending one's motivation to act into a spiral. One must have the courage to face an unsensational reality, to have an insatiable interest in the world. Because of the melancholy that results from faint-heartedness in the face of the overwhelming offers in the mass media, the conflict between the will to participate in the world and one's limitations, the need for unaware and sealed-off isolation during the production process, one's vulnerability because of being open and exposed, and the experience of occasional volatile euphoria when things are flowing successfully through one's raster seemingly without effort, one must take care not to become overextended and that the amount and incomprehensibility of the material does not get out of hand. The unavoidable presence of fear caused by the uncertain denouement increasingly weighs one down. Sometimes concentrating on the act of production helps.

The possibility of the opposite's happening comes about at the moment of ascertainment. The more observations and information are processed, the more that remains unsaid. One formulates a personal position from a swimming pool of possibilities, synchronising it with a prolific forest of existing signals and all the other systems of forms in circulation that have been derived from them, are self-referential, or have been artificially produced. A position that is active, anti-individualistic, and socially responsible adopts the defiant position necessary to counter the multiplied hysteria of the mass media with one's own images, in spite of the evidence that such a policy is extremely limited and certainly doomed to fail. This is activity, instead of mere rejection, that criticises the everyday barrage of prefabricated visual footage by juxtaposing even more images. A certain feeling of release can be found through the act itself and its integration in established strategies: implanting a small monotone sing-song in a mass culture that specialises in presenting the spectacular highs of exceptional cases and quickly absorbing every other voice.

6)
Chuck Palahniuk: *Diary*

What you don't understand can mean anything … Because everything is important.
Every detail. We just don`t know why yet. 6)

One seeks to explain the internal processes
of thinking and working using real-life material as an
axis of rotation for a description of an individual cos-
mos; propounding the viscid normality and triviality
of life, without the heights and depths of memorable
incidents, and recreating and exposing the many aspects, influences, rituals, and daily routines as realisti-
cally as possible – such as with fragments of stories,
parenthetical observations, rudiments of linearity,
abstract closeness, interacting levels and layers, and
the visual mirrorings of one's mind. Is it possible that
a report of personal occurrences accomplishes more
than the limitations of a patchy draft and connects
with the viewer in a more abstractly comprehensible
general semiology?

7)
Samuel Beckett: *Proust*

Reality, whether you approach it through your
imagination or empirically, remains a surface,
hermetically sealed. 7)

Everybody has at least the potential possibility
of actively participating in the world by contributing
opinions derived from personal experiences and influences. How does the external world make itself apparent to one's eyes and arrest one's attention while one
is at the same time conscious of the difficult position
of being a part of this very world? In extending one's
own knowledge of the world, one aims to impart that
knowledge without the arrogance of thinking that
easy, bold, and strikingly satisfactory answers can be
found. One describes one's own personal relational
system in order not to differentiate, but to integrate
oneself and to understand to what extent captured
temporary results make sense to the other person and
how information can be proffered and transported.

Unfolding the external conditions of life, one
attempts to ascertain if inscrutable internal processes
can be used as a method: in working with the material
and loading it with meaning by means of selection,
one then institutes a test situation that defines the
parameters, which involve a preconceived timeframe,
a determined space and radius of action, a fast and
somehow automatic succession and production, and
an established vocabulary.

In trying to create a transfer of positions from
an individual to the collective memory within the
established medium of a book, before any information
can be stored, it must first be codified: a transformation
of the visible into a metalayer of open symbols, which
the recipient is then able to read. The subjectivity of
that which is seen is transformed into intersubjectivity
– the duality between subject and object disappears
with the examination of their relationship. The person
of the author remains secondary in the process of
transcription, although important questions are treated
involving thought and work processes that integrate
and combine the conscious and unconscious imposing
themselves: making an image is a conscious and con-
trolled action that implies the existence of an autonomous subject. Nevertheless, decisions taken within
the production process are at the same time submitted
to an unconscious and mysteriously veiled process of
intuition.

When relating the different layers and levels of consciousness between the world itself and the interpretation of it, and between image-maker and recipient, while overcoming the differences in their social, cultural, or intellectual backgrounds, is it possible to transfer personal experience from one person to another without being intractable and exerting force and undue influence? One can only offer a number of possibilities of subjects to be dealt with, hinting at potential ways of reading and interpreting them. More than merely offering visual impressions in a lookbook displaying a materialisation of concrete and less concrete thoughts that come into being at the moment an item is perceived or committed to memory, an attempt has been made to invite the recipient not to resign from the world in frustration because of the latter's complexity, but to continue and engage him or herself, accepting and learning about the world in its manifoldness, developing an understanding of its impulses and the brilliance of the material it has to offer, always sharpening his or her sense of awareness. Unanswered questions are inevitable and preferred to didactic opinions.

The amount of non-knowledge increases exponentially with each acquisition of new knowledge. The essence of a thing is probably not immediately obvious, but lies behind what is apparent at first glance: When daily rituals and routines become automatic and one no longer consciously thinks about what one is seeing or doing, space is established in one's mind for something to happen. An uncompromising and continuous approach from all sides and a questioning scrutiny in dealing with the subject will most likely lead to more significant results than a direct, frontal approach. Things become surprisingly more interesting when they do not impose themselves offensively and do not open out and reveal all at first glance. Decisions about their relevance are taken on many levels, are never final, and result from being continuously dealt with, at best in a sleepwalk-like metastate of parenthetical approximation, similar to the moment when one attunes to intuition.

How are we constituted as subject of our own knowledge? How are we constituted as subjects who exercise or submit to power relations? How are we constituted as moral subjects of our own actions? 2)

The true beginning of scientific activity consists rather in describing phenomena and then in proceeding to group, classify and correlate them. Even at the state of description it is not possible to avoid applying certain abstract ideas to the material in hand, ideas derived from somewhere or other but certainly not from the new observations alone. Such ideas – which will later become the basic concepts of science – are still more indispensable as the material is further worked over. They must at first necessarily possess some degree of indefiniteness; there can be no question of any clear delimitation of their content. So long as they remain in this condition, we come to an understanding about their meaning by making repeated references to the material of observation from which they appear to have been derived, but upon which, in fact, they have been imposed. Thus, strictly speaking, they are in the nature of conventions – although everything depends on their not being arbitrarily chosen but determined by their having significant relations to the empirical material, relations that we seem to sense before we can clearly recognise and demonstrate them. It is only after more thorough investigation of the field of observation that we are able to formulate its basic scientific concepts with increased precision, and progressively so to modify them that they become serviceable and consistent over a wide area. 3)

2)
Michel Foucault: Résumé des cours, taken from *The Foucault Reader* (trans. Paul Rabinow)

3)
Jacques Lacan: *The Seminar of Jacques Lacan: Book II: The Ego in Freud's Theory and in the Technique of Psychoanalysis 1954-1955 (Seminar of Jacques Lacan)* (trans. Sylvana Tomaselli)

Searching with open senses for similarities, connections, counterparts to and friction points with one's own thoughts, mindsets, memories, and approach to the outside world, thus establishing a basis for them to evolve using the visual language of the existing external material – when one discovers matches, it engenders feelings of hope, confidence, and affiliation with and embeddedness in the world and defines a mutual frame of reference that offers and establishes a convergence and a relationship with the world.

Arranging elements of reality into a scientific test structure, evaluating the systematic order that is taken as a basis for the perception of things, making use of the available technical tools and possibilities, working quickly and roughly simulating and approximating real conditions as closely as possible, facing the paradoxical situation of transcribing the material into arbitrary systems of meaning with the goal of finding something out about the world, while moving about, restless and intertwined with its field of force – one is operating within the system one is a part of without having the amenity of an external, autonomous position of retreat. The method of investigation used sometimes causes the results to become obscured rather than elucidated, which nevertheless occasionally leads to a diffuse intuitive clarity.

1)
Paul McCarthy: *Art Now 2*

It is my belief that our culture has lost a true perception of existence. It is veiled. We are only tumbling in what we perceive to be reality. For the most part we do not know we are alive. 1)

As a way of accounting for existence, an exercise in remembrance, and a description of the mechanical and stereotypical everyday processes of life, the method itself contains a theory about the examined and consists of a manic appropriation and production of corresponding visual imagery. Repetitive attempts sometimes lead to a claustrophobic density of description; other attempts remain transient and volatile, expecting further execution. One attempts to establish a comprehensible access to the world with the inherent knowledge that more than a strictly rational understanding, only a serene acceptance of whatever happens remains. The developed images are frozen moments dependent upon the medium: their fixation and stillness is beguiling, and their seemingly definitiveness simulates an untenable, peaceful reality.

Embedded in a wholeness, each element expresses itself in but a brief, transient, and intimate moment, referring simultaneously to the past and the future and to the structural proportions of power in a world that is not self-contained, harmonious, and balanced, but one that is perpetually changing, providing no security because no form and no statement has an assigned place within that world. The present sequence of images provides – in contrast to collections of snapshots in a family album, photographs of sights, or postcard motifs (preserved mostly for a future probe of elapsed better times) – concrete possibilities for present action

4)
Michel Foucault: What Is an Author? in *Language, Counter-Memory, Practice* (trans. Donald F. Bouchard and Sherry Simon)

Under what conditions and through what forms can an entity like the subject appear in the order of discourse; what position does it occupy; what functions does it exhibit; and what rules does it follow in each type of discourse? In short, the subject (and its substitutes) must be stripped of its creative role and analysed as a complex and variable function of discourse. 4)

D1734752

<u>we have no scar to show for happiness</u>

Persistently appraising the surrounding environment by means of a collection of random but not arbitrary pieces of information; sifting through the material, trying to apprehend the perception process and the procedure of transmitting and communicating the data obtained.